OLYMPIC MOUNTAIN PURSUIT

JODIE BAILEY

LOVE INSPIRED SUSPENSE

INSPIRATIONAL ROMANCE

Special thanks and acknowledgment are given to Jodie Bailey for her contribution to the Pacific Northwest K-9 Unit miniseries.

LOVE INSPIRED® SUSPENSE

INSPIRATIONAL ROMANCE

Recycling programs for this product may not exist in your area.

ISBN-13: 978-1-335-58780-0

Olympic Mountain Pursuit

For questions and comments about the quality of this book, please contact us at CustomerService@Harlequin.com.

Love Inspired
22 Adelaide St. West, 41st Floor
Toronto, Ontario M5H 4E3, Canada
www.LoveInspired.com

Printed in U.S.A.

To appoint unto them that mourn in Zion, to give
unto them beauty for ashes, the oil of joy for mourning,
the garment of praise for the spirit of heaviness;
that they might be called trees of righteousness,
the planting of the Lord, that he might be glorified.
—*Isaiah* 61:3

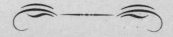

To Laura Ott,

For being the most selfless and the most patient

For sharing my OBX-loving heart

For cheering me on when I'm ready to quit

Oh, and for making the best desserts in the world.

(All my beach people said "Amen"...)

ONE

The sound of the east fork of the Quinault River raging against the rocks in the narrow gorge was louder than Everly Lopez had ever heard it.

She lowered her binoculars to give her eyes a rest. She'd spent all day in the dense foliage of Olympic National Park, tracking black bears. With the Pony Bridge Trail and several others in Enchanted Valley closed due to washouts and high water from unusually heavy rains, animal activity was increasing in the absence of hikers and park visitors.

The quiet was nice, a return to her refuge after a harrowing season during which a series of bombings had wreaked terror in the park. With the bomber now in custody, Everly finally felt as though she could relax again in the one place that always felt safe.

She'd been on her way back to the trailhead when she'd spotted a large male black bear chasing a cougar away from a downed deer near Pony Bridge. Black bears were known for stealing a kill, and watching these two battle for their lunch had distracted her from her own safety. While it was still early in the afternoon, Enchanted Valley was growing dark from clouds and the mist that always seemed to hang in the rain forest.

It was time to pack it in for the day and make the two-plus-mile hike back to the trailhead. Everly's friend Tara kept her daughter, Amelia, during the day and, if Everly headed in early, maybe she could go for a late lunch to a fast-food place with a playground. It would be a treat for them all.

One more peek, then she had to get moving. It was tough to leave, but the weather didn't give her much choice. Not only was the data she was collecting as a Black Bear Habitat and Outreach tech going to help the Department of Fish and Wildlife, it was also going a long way toward bolstering her research for her PhD in environmental science.

With a slight grin, Everly raised her binoculars and scanned the lush green underbrush and trees until she found the bear again, now resting on his backside and staring in her direction.

Had he spotted her? Everly stilled, grateful for the bear spray in a holster at her hip but praying she wouldn't have to use it.

Something rustled in the trees behind her and she whipped around, lowering her binoculars. With cougars emboldened by a lack of foot traffic on the trail, she should have been watching her back. While the big cats rarely attacked humans, they wouldn't be shy about it if they were hungry enough.

Letting her binoculars dangle at her neck, she grabbed the bear spray from its holster and prepared to act as the aggressor. Hopefully, the critter would back down without her having to deploy spray in its face.

Her grip faltered when she faced her would-be attacker, but her fingers tightened just in time to keep a hold on the canister. This was no rain forest animal from the Cascade Mountains.

This was a man.

And he was pointing a gun at her.

Everly's foot slipped on a mossy rock as she instinctively stepped back, lifting her hands. Her mouth went dry. "Can I— What do—" The words required force to bypass the lump in her throat. "What do you want?"

The man maintained his position about twenty feet from her, but he adjusted his grip to center the pistol's aim on her chest. "I want you." The matter-of-fact tone made the words even more chilling.

Her breath stuttered. Her knees threatened to drop her to the hard-packed trail. She was alone out here. With the trails closed, no one would hear her if she screamed. No one would come to her rescue. It was just her, this man and a rapidly darkening sky.

If only that bear would suddenly attack...

Bear. She was still holding the spray, which was nothing more than industrial-strength pepper spray with a thirty-foot range. She glanced at the canister in her chilled fingers then back to the man. If she could turn the canister a half inch, then she'd be able to—

"I wouldn't if I were you." He stepped closer, his blue eyes icy beneath military-short blond hair. He wore jeans and a dark blue windbreaker, likely to ward off the damp mist and approaching rain. "This might only be a tranquilizer gun, but I promise you it will hurt. Also, you don't want me to carry you out of here over my shoulder, because the more trouble you make for me, the more I make for you, Dr. Ward."

Everly's eyes widened as she gasped. *Ward.* She hadn't been Dr. Everly Ward for over four years. Not

since her husband was murdered. Not since she'd testi-
fied against Kassandra Rennish, the human trafficker
who'd pulled the trigger when she discovered Noah was
gathering evidence to be used against her.

Kassandra had smiled directly at Everly as she'd been
led from the courtroom, and Everly had known even
before the verbal threat…the woman would do all she
could to destroy her.

That was the reason she'd accepted a new life for herself and her daughter in the witness protection program,
away from her home and family and all that she knew.

But now she'd been found.

She had to get out of this forest and back to her
daughter. Then she had to do the unthinkable… To call
the US marshal assigned to her case and let him know
that death was no longer stalking her.

It had found her.

But first, she had to save herself from the man who
was casually leveling a tranquilizer dart at her heart.

Bear spray worked on bears, but so did a show of
authority. Maybe it would work on this man. If she
bucked up to him, maybe she could distract him long
enough to use the one weapon she had at her disposal.
If he'd wanted to tranquilize her, he'd have already done
it. Chances were high he'd do everything in his power
not to haul her dead weight along a two-and-a-half-
mile trail on foot.

A drop splashed her temple and slid down her cheek.

In the rain.

He tilted his head, glancing at the sky then back to
her. "Put the bear spray down, and this will be easier
on both of us."

"Why would I do that?"

As more drops fell between them, the man hefted a heavy sigh as though she bored him. "Because I get an extra ten thousand if I bring you in alive." He reached behind him at his waist and pulled something forward with his left hand.

A pistol.

Everly froze.

He aimed the gun straight for her heart. "But I still get a payday if I prove you're dead. Don't make me decide that ten thousand isn't worth the hassle of dragging you out of here."

Everly's pulse pounded in her head so hard that dark spots rhythmically throbbed in her vision. She was going to pass out. When she did, he'd probably kill her and move on to save himself.

She had one shot. One chance to get back to her daughter.

"Okay." Slowly, she leaned forward as though she was going to lay the bear spray on the ground, rotating the canister slightly as she did. She flicked the safety with her thumb and pressed the lever.

The man howled like a wounded bear and dropped both of his weapons, clawing at his face.

Everly turned and bolted toward the trailhead. It was two and a half miles of slippery rocks and narrow path, but she had a head start she was determined to keep.

She was two paces away when the skies opened up, the oversaturated ground allowing the water to run in an instant creek along the trail. The weather would slow her getaway, but she couldn't let it stop her. Salvation lay with her vehicle in the trailhead parking lot.

Up ahead was the wooden Pony Bridge about fifteen feet over the narrow gorge, where the swollen Quinault

River surged beneath. Normally only a few feet deep, the water was running incredibly high now, the current strong. Past that, there was nothing but forest between her and the parking lot. She didn't dare slow to see if her phone had a signal. She just needed to get out.

As her foot hit the bridge, heavy footsteps crashed through the brush behind her.

He was coming, and he'd be raging mad from the pain.

She was halfway across the bridge when another figure materialized out of the rain in front of her, blocking her path. His raised hood shadowed his face, and the rain obscured his form. "Everly!"

She skidded to a halt, her foot sliding on wet wooden slats, taking her down to her knee before she scrambled up. One man behind. One man before.

The river beneath.

Jumping could kill her. Though the current was swift, the water wasn't deep enough to support a dive.

Still, she'd take her chances with nature over humans every time.

Climbing onto the slippery rail, she leaped, curling into a ball as the man called her name again. She thought she heard a dog barking as her body slammed into the surging water.

What had—

Had Everly just jumped?

Pacific Northwest K-9 Unit Officer Jackson Dean glanced after his partner, a Doberman named Rex, who was barreling across Pony Bridge. The protection K-9 had obeyed Jackson's shouted command and raced toward the man who'd chased Everly Lopez out of the forest. Rex's deep bark said he was still in pursuit.

But Everly had gone over the wooden rail and into the river.

Did he back up his partner or rescue the witness as he'd been assigned?

Jackson evaluated the swiftly rushing water. Several yards downstream, Everly surfaced, then dove again. It was tough to determine if she was trying to hide or if she was struggling in the unusually high water.

He couldn't let her drown. Couldn't watch someone else he was supposed to be protecting die.

Especially not Everly.

Kicking off his shoes and shucking off his backpack, Jackson gauged the river's depth and jumped, tucking his knees into his chest as he hit the water, chilled by mountain runoff even in July. His lower back grazed rocks at the bottom and he straightened his legs, pushing toward the surface. He charged forward with the roiling current, searching for Everly. Several days of flooding rains had swollen the Quinault, which charged angrily through the narrow gorge. The surging water and pounding rain from the deluge that once again fell from the sky was deafening.

Fighting to keep his head above the water and to shield his body from the gorge's rocky walls, Jackson scanned for evidence that Everly had surfaced again. He prayed for a small beach, though any that typically existed were probably under several feet of water.

There. To the right. A narrow trail led up from where a thin strip of land usually existed. The river ebbed in the hollow of the rock, quieter away from the current and as it spread over a small cove.

Everly Lopez stood in water up to her knees, scanning the river with fear-filled eyes. Her dark hair hung in streaming rivulets, clinging to her cheeks. Her jeans and green T-shirt were soaked.

As soon as she spotted Jackson through the torrential rain, she turned and tried to run for the trail, the water slowing her progress. It had been clear that, in her panic, she hadn't recognized him.

Jackson made a shallow dive and plunged forward. He had to reach her. There was no way of knowing how many of Kassandra Rennish's hit men were roaming Olympic National Park in search of Everly. The young mother's testimony as an eyewitness to her husband's murder had put an end to Rennish's transnational trafficking operation. But the moment Kassandra had escaped from prison, she'd probably redoubled her efforts to locate Everly.

If so, that meant any number of Rennish's killers could be searching for Everly, intent on a payday.

Adrenaline drove Jackson forward, and he hit the shallow water near the beach, scrambling to his feet.

Everly had just reached the rocky trail and was struggling to gain a foothold.

"Everly! Stop!" He tried to race forward against the river's current, but the water was like running through wet concrete. He reached her as she started climbing and grabbed the back of her shirt. "Everly, it's me. Jackson Dean."

She twisted and fought as he dragged her away from the rock face. As her feet splashed into the water again, she found her footing and ripped away from him, rounding on him with fire in her eyes. Her fist flew, and Jackson barely had time to step sideways. The blow caught him in the shoulder, and he stumbled back.

Whoa. The woman had strength. She'd definitely

done some working out since he'd last seen her. The Everly he'd protected when he was in the Marshals Service hadn't possessed that kind of physical power.

Rotating his shoulder against the blow, he reached into his collar and pulled out the Pacific Northwest K-9 Unit badge he wore on a chain around his neck. "Everly." He tried to keep his voice even. Yelling at her earlier probably hadn't been the best course of action, but he had to get her moving. She could be in a sniper's crosshairs even now. The thought made his skin crawl. "It's really me. Jackson Dean." She had to recognize him. They'd been through a lot together.

Everly's eyes went wide and she backed away until she was against the rocks, holding tight as the current tugged at her knees. "You don't look like him." She shook her head and, to add to the twist in Jackson's gut, tears filled her eyes. "I don't care who sent you, just please…don't kill me. My family has been through enough."

Letting the badge fall against his chest, Jackson held up both hands. She'd never seen him soaking wet or with the beard he'd grown since he joined the PNK9 team. In her panic, she probably wouldn't even recognize herself in the mirror, let alone a man she hadn't seen in four years.

He had one more piece of information. One more way to prove he was who he claimed to be. "I was at the hospital when your daughter, Amelia, was born." Surely she remembered? He'd been her point of contact, practically a constant in her life.

This time when her eyes widened, it was in recognition. "Jackson?" She stepped closer. Her voice trembled, probably from the chilled water as much as from fear. "Why are you here? You left the Marshals. Left—"

Us. She was going to say *us.*

There wasn't time to talk about that. He had to get her to safety. He needed to return to Rex and make sure his partner was safe. This was no time for a reunion. "Deputy Marshal Collin Anderson fell off the grid two days ago. That's why I'm here." Anderson had been assigned as Everly's point of contact when Jackson left the service. Anderson hadn't answered his phone, nor had he been into the office. A search of his home had come up empty. Even his vehicle was missing.

Jackson didn't want to think about what that could mean, especially since Kassandra Rennish had escaped when members of her organization ambushed a prison transfer eight days earlier. With Rennish in the wind, Anderson missing and Everly facing off against a thug in the deep forest…they could be facing the worst-case scenario every protected witness had nightmares about.

"Deputy Marshal Anderson has always been quick to answer if I needed anything, even if I was just feeling paranoid. Something's wrong." Everly looked upstream and down, then over her shoulder at the steep climb to the top of the gorge. "That man on the bridge knew who I was."

"I know." When PNK9 Chief Donovan Fanelli had informed him the Marshals wanted him to track down Everly in the rain forest, Jackson had already assumed the worst. Learning that Anderson was missing had doubled down his resolve to find her. Knowing she'd already faced the barrel of a gun had him past the edge.

He had to get her to safety until a team from the Marshals Service could relocate her.

One thing at a time, though. Now that he'd calmed Everly down and made certain she was safe, he wanted nothing more than to get back to his partner. "I'm with the Pacific Northwest K-9 Unit, a specialized law enforcement team assigned to Washington's national parks. My K-9 partner, Rex, is trained in protection. I sent him after the guy who came at you, and I'm hoping Rex took him down, but I have no way of knowing if he did or where your attacker is now. I'd really like to know Rex is okay, if you're ready to start moving."

Jackson had texted for backup as soon as he'd come upon Everly and her attacker. Officers Isaac McDane and Danica Hayes should be on their way, but there was no telling how long it would take them to get to the trailhead or to hike the trail with rain pouring down over them.

He felt for his phone to send an update.

The holster was empty. He turned a slow circle, searching the water at his feet. No phone. *Great.* Chances were high that he'd lost it in the river. It would have been toast anyway after the dunking he'd just endured. "Did your cell survive the plunge?" It was a long shot, but maybe—

"I don't know." Everly patted her hip pocket, then checked the others. "It's probably in the water. Cell service is hit or miss out here and, given we're below the walls of the gorge, it wouldn't help you anyway." Worry lines creased her forehead. "My daughter… She's with a friend, but…"

There was no need for her to finish the sentence. They were in the wilderness without communication, and she was cut off from her child. "Let's move."

Everly was making her way up the slick rock trail

before Jackson could say more. He had no doubt she wanted to reach Amelia even more than he wanted to get back to his partner, who was alone on the trail with an armed man.

Thankfully, he hadn't heard a gunshot, but between the roar of the river and the pounding of the rain, they'd have been hard-pressed to hear anything.

At the top of the riverbank, Everly scrambled onto flat ground and waited for him before she headed along the narrow path that wound above the river through dense green underbrush. In the rain forest, trails had to be used daily or they became overgrown quickly. Recent closures in the park had given plants an opportunity to reclaim ground lost to the footsteps of more humans than the Park Service could count.

They reached Pony Bridge faster than he'd anticipated, given that it felt as though they'd been in the river for hours. He prayed Rex was safe and had been able to hold the suspect at bay.

The deluge began to taper off as they stepped onto the rain-slicked boards of Pony Bridge.

Jackson tucked Everly behind him and rested his hand on his pistol, grateful it had remained strapped in its holster during the excitement. It was wet but it should operate just fine if he needed it.

He prayed he wouldn't need it.

Reaching down, he picked up his backpack and passed it to her instead of taking the time to put it back on. "Stay behind me, no matter what. If this goes south, run and I'll cover you."

He hoped she heard him, because she made no sound.

Crossing the open expanse of the bridge with Everly

wasn't his ideal choice, but there was no way he was leaving her without protection.

He strained to hear above the water rushing beneath them or the rain dripping from the trees, but it was impossible. "Rex, speak!"

There was no answering bark.

"Do you think he's okay?" Everly's voice was low, but her concern was evident. She'd been a veterinarian before disappearing into WITSEC. Animals held her heart. Setting her up to work toward another doctorate and to study forest creatures had been a natural fit.

Jackson didn't have the heart to answer her question. He also didn't have the heart to consider that everything might not be *okay*.

As they reached the other side of the bridge, something orange caught his eye beside the trail. Kneeling, he picked it up. Everly's bear spray. He passed it to her, admiring the bravery it had taken for her to defend herself.

As they stepped deeper into the tree line, Jackson slowed and drew his weapon. The trail was too rocky and too wet to hold prints of any kind, but he walked slowly, searching. The sound of the river had muted behind them before he saw what he dreaded most.

Rex, collapsed in the center of the trail, motionless.

TWO

Everly gasped and jogged behind Jackson as he dropped to the dog's side, running his hands over soaking wet fur. *Please, God, let Rex be okay.* She could handle a lot of things, *had* handled a lot of things, but a murdered animal would be beyond her capacity to deal with today.

She set Jackson's backpack on the ground. This was her wheelhouse. The old Everly Ward had been a large animal veterinarian, heading up a practice near Houston. She could certainly handle examining Jackson's K-9.

If only Everly Lopez could still tap into Everly Ward. It had been so long…

She knelt beside Jackson. Despite her stress and fear, she had to try to help them both. "Can I check on Rex? If you remember, I used to be a vet." Cows and horses had been her typical clients, but she was certain she could aid the Doberman. She just had to think smaller. "The guy who came after me had a tranquilizer gun, so maybe…" There was no visible blood, so hopefully he'd used it instead of the pistol. And hopefully those darts had been loaded for her weight and not for a bear's weight. An overdose of sedative could have already signed Rex's death warrant.

Everly swallowed panic at the idea of someone meticulously dosing a dart to her specifications. Shuddering, she shook off that thought and focused on the dog as Jackson slid to the side in the mud.

"Please?" He shielded Rex's head from the smattering of raindrops that dripped from trees and sky.

Moving into the spot Jackson had vacated, Everly scanned the dog. Rex was a gorgeous animal, dark and sleek, with the tan patches that gave the breed their traditional look. Whoever had raised and trained him had thankfully left his ears and tail natural instead of docking them, a practice Everly had always been opposed to. "I'll take a look at your dog, and—"

"*Partner.* Rex is my partner."

"Right. Your partner." She should have remembered that. K-9s were considered officers just like any human would be. In fact, Rex's black harness was emblazoned with *PNK9* in bold letters and an official identification tag.

She ran her hands over his short fur, finding no signs of bullet or blood. When she paused to evaluate his heartbeat and respirations, both were steady and strong, though his breathing was shallow due to his slumber. If she hadn't known better, she'd think he was simply a deep-sleeping dog.

But where had the dart struck?

She ran her hands under his shoulder, and her fingers grazed something fuzzy. "Lift his head a little."

Expression knit with concern, Jackson gently raised Rex's head.

Everly reached beneath and slipped a dart from his shoulder just above the harness. "The guy had good aim. He caught Rex about an inch from where the harness would have offered some protection. It seems that, based on Rex's heart rate and respiration, the dart wasn't loaded for bear but for—" she held up the red-feathered dart between them and attempted to keep the emotion from her voice "—for a smaller animal."

Jackson eased Rex's head to the ground and met Everly's eyes over the animal. "By that you mean a human. You."

Everly dug her teeth into her lower lip.

"I doubt we'll find much evidence on it thanks to the mud and rain, but we'll take it in." He reached for his backpack and pulled out an evidence kit, carefully depositing the dart into a plastic bag, then sealing it before he shoved it into the pack.

Sitting back on his heels, Jackson stared up the trail. "What I can't figure out was what he planned to do if he'd shot you with that thing. It probably wouldn't have put you under, but it definitely would have slowed you down. Was he going to haul you out of the forest in a fireman's carry across his shoulders? It's over two miles back to the trailhead. If he came in from the direction he stepped out of the woods, it's a much longer, much more intense hike."

"I guess he was hoping I wouldn't resist."

"Or, somewhere out there, he's got some sort of help. I just don't..." Jackson looked down at his unconscious partner and seemed to shake something off. "Can he be moved?"

"I obviously can't make you any guarantees, but I don't see why not. Depending on what was in the sedative, he could wake up while you're carrying him though. Sometimes animals come out of anesthesia disoriented and aggressive."

"I'll take my chances." Jackson shouldered his backpack and then, with Everly's help, hoisted Rex onto his shoulders. He turned toward the bridge as the rain finally came to an end. A distant rumble of thunder and the swollen clouds overhead threatened another deluge as the afternoon light dimmed. "I want to get you out of here. There's no telling where your attacker is now, and the last thing we need is him getting the drop on us out here while we're tending to Rex."

Tension clenched Everly's shoulders and she stood suddenly, scanning the trees. For a moment, taking care of the dog, she'd forgotten that the man could still be watching them, especially if he thought he'd neutralized his greatest threat when he'd taken out the animal.

Jackson shifted his grip on Rex's legs. "Let's go. I've got backup headed our way. The more ground we cover the faster we'll meet them, but I'm guessing the trail is in worse condition than before." He tipped his chin for her to go ahead of him and followed with Rex, moving slowly and stopping every hundred feet or so, probably to listen for sounds behind them.

All Everly could hear was the dripping of water from the trees and the forest animals scurrying back to life now that the rain had passed. Thunder quickened her steps, though. The last place she wanted to be was in the woods with an assassin on her trail while lightning threatened to blitz them off the map faster than any man could.

She only had the capacity to fear one thing right now, nature or humans. She couldn't handle the stress of worrying about both. Nature was something she understood and could protect herself from.

Unfortunately, she also understood the violence of humans all too well.

Everly kept putting one foot in front of the other. Behind her, Jackson puffed under the weight of his partner's body. The last time she'd seen the then-deputy marshal, she had just settled into her first apartment in Olympia, and he'd told her he was handing her care over to Deputy Marshal Collin Anderson. All she'd been able to gather was that something had happened on another case, and he was leaving the Marshals Service for good.

His sudden departure had rocked her newly built foundation. For months, he'd been a constant in her life, the head of her case as she transitioned into WITSEC. He'd been her point of contact when she'd gone to Washington, DC, for orientation. He'd been the one to answer all of her questions and to act as a sounding board when she grew frightened or frustrated.

When she'd gone into premature labor on the move out to Washington State, he'd made certain she was safe at the hospital in Sioux Falls, South Dakota. Jackson had been the one pacing the waiting room as she underwent an emergency C-section. When an infection nearly killed her and caused complications that had kept both her and Amelia hospitalized for more than a week, it had been Jackson who made sure they were cared for and had everything they needed.

She almost smiled. He'd even changed quite a few diapers when Everly was too weak to do so.

Jackson Dean had been so much more to her, though. He'd been the one to awkwardly hug her when the tears came frequently over the grief of a husband murdered before he even knew Everly was carrying his only child.

In those dark days, comfort and protection and help had all come from Jackson.

Her foot slipped on a rock and she righted herself quickly, moving forward as the sky continued to grow more threatening. Water dripping from the thick trees into the even thicker underbrush obscured most sounds, and she was grateful Jackson was behind her, listening and watching.

She should probably be paying more attention to her surroundings but focusing on the past was the one thing that kept her from panicking about the present. Because if she'd been identified, she'd have to leave this life behind and start all over again. She'd lived in fear of such a moment.

Her heart seemed to shudder. Everly laid a hand on her chest, where a gold filigree cross hung beneath her shirt on a long chain. That, too, had come from Jackson. Along with a Bible, it had been his gift to her after he helped her come to know the God and His Son Whom he'd prayed to so often on her behalf.

Everything he'd done for her, including giving her that cross and the Bible, had likely violated a thousand protocols, but he'd been a lifeline to both her and to Amelia.

He'd been a friend…

Until he left the Marshals and never contacted them again. The rules dictated that he couldn't, not without jeopardizing her safety and his own.

Deputy Marshal Anderson, whom she spoke with on rare occasions, was by-the-book and all business. Their interactions were different but also as they should be.

And now he was missing. "Nobody has heard from Deputy Marshal Anderson?"

"No." The word was clipped.

Either he didn't want to talk about it or the burden of hauling his partner along the trail was heavier than Everly had initially thought.

If only she could—

Something crashed through the underbrush ahead of them around the bend. Instinctively, Everly reached for her bear spray before remembering she'd emptied the can on her attacker.

Another heavy sound came as rain drizzled down again, foretelling a coming storm.

Something, or someone, was coming straight for them, and there was nowhere to hide.

Jackson widened his stance and shifted Rex's weight across his shoulders, fighting for balance on the trail as he rested his hand on his gun. There was no cover. While the underbrush was thick and green and the trees stood close to the trail, they offered little protection from someone searching for them. "Everly," he hissed at her, hoping that whoever was coming was his backup and that, if they weren't, they wouldn't hear him. "Get behind me."

She squeezed past him on the trail, standing close to his back.

It felt as though Rex was suddenly a few pounds lighter. She must be helping to hold some of his weight.

She'd make a great partner if he ever wanted a human one.

Had he seriously just thought that? Now?

Jackson forced himself to focus on what might soon be a fight to the death. As his fingers flicked the latch on his holster and wrapped around the grip of his side-arm, two figures rounded the bend in the trail.

Jackson's hold relaxed and his shoulders sagged before he remembered he was carrying Rex. Instantly, he straightened before his partner could shift position. "It's okay. The cavalry is here."

Officer Isaac McDane and his partner, Freddy, a beagle trained in electronics detection, appeared. Close behind him on the narrow trail was Officer Danica Hayes and her partner, Hutch, a German shepherd trained in suspect apprehension.

Danica passed Isaac and hurried forward with Hutch, resting a hand on Rex's head. "Is he okay?"

"Everly says his pulse and breathing seem good, but he needs a vet. He was hit with a tranquilizer dart that was meant for Everly." That was another thing he was going to have to think about later, after they were safely out of the literal woods. The idea of someone firing a tranquilizer dart at her made his blood ice.

Leaving her hand on Rex's head, Danica looked to Everly. "You're the witness Jackson was sent to protect?"

"I am." Her voice was soft behind him, almost at the breaking point. Now that they had backup, it almost sounded as though her emotions were about to get the better of her.

They probably were. Her daughter was with a friend, unprotected and out of reach.

But not anymore. Isaac would have a phone on him. As Everly stepped to his side, Jackson looked at her, angling his neck to see past Rex. "Do you know your babysitter's phone number?"

"No. She's a good friend, but once I put her number

in my phone I never looked at it again." Her chin came up. "I can give you her address, though."

Perfect. "Isaac, if you can get a signal, can you call and have someone get to the address Everly gives you? Have them make contact but stand back and watch after that. We don't want to alarm the babysitter, but if someone has come after Everly, we want to be sure there's no threat elsewhere." There almost definitely would be. If Kassandra Rennish wanted to destroy Everly's life, she wouldn't hesitate to make a run at Amelia in order to do it.

No way was he saying that right now, but they did need to get moving. As Everly stepped around him to speak to Isaac, he looked to Danica, whose hand still rested on Rex's head. "How much farther to the trail-head?"

"We were walking as fast as conditions would allow and it was about half an hour. You're toting Rex, so it might be longer."

"I can move faster than you think." Thunder punctuated his assertion. "Let's go."

The group moved forward with Danica in the lead and Isaac bringing up the rear. With extra eyes and ears, Jackson relaxed a bit, focusing on the job of carrying his partner to safety.

Safety. It had been a rare thing in the park lately. He'd just come off an assignment with Willow Bates and her once-and-future husband, Theo, tracking a bomber in the park. With the bomber's arrest, Jackson had hoped to feel safe in the forest and mountains once again. He hadn't counted on having to go on the run from an assassin so soon after defeating danger the first time.

Everly walked in front of him, and he tried not to

study the back of her head too hard, to keep his focus on the trail instead.

But plodding through the rain forest didn't keep his mind occupied enough to stop the memories. He'd been assigned to her case when she was moved to DC for orientation. Everly had been seven months pregnant following the trial, grieving the loss of her husband who'd been murdered by Kassandra Rennish and traumatized over having to uproot her life in the aftermath of her testimony.

While Jackson typically kept emotional distance from witnesses, Everly's intense vulnerability had touched something inside him. His sister had been pregnant at the time as well, only due a few weeks ahead of Everly. At first, that had been the thing that made him want to protect her more fully.

But as time passed, he'd begun to view her as a friend, and then…

And then he'd crossed a line. A line he'd never told her or anyone else about. He'd started to feel more for her. To want to protect her as something beyond a marshal or a friend. Everly was warm and funny when she wasn't terrified. Intelligent and loyal and dedicated. Under other circumstances, Jackson would have asked her out, would have attempted to get to know her better.

But she'd been a grieving widow in a traumatic situation, and that would never have been appropriate, even if he hadn't been assigned to protect her.

When she'd gone into premature labor during her transfer, he'd paced the waiting room, praying through her C-section and through the infection that had nearly killed her in the aftermath. He'd been on the scene to help her with Amelia and to tell her about how Jesus had sustained him throughout his life.

He'd desperately needed God two months later, when a witness under his protection, Lance Carnalle, had been killed by a car bomb before he could testify against his boss, a Texas businessman accused of racketeering and human trafficking.

That explosion had rocked Jackson to his core. Although Jackson had repeatedly warned him, Carnalle had violated protocol by slipping away and going to the hospital to see his mother, who had undergone heart bypass surgery.

Jackson should have seen it coming. He should have taken extra precautions to make sure Carnalle stayed put. Nobody saw the man going to such extraordinary lengths to get to that hospital.

But Jackson should have. It was his job to pay attention.

He would never make that mistake again.

Isaac's voice behind him drew Jackson out of his reverie. He was finally passing along the address Everly had given him earlier. *Good.* Amelia would be safe. That little baby he'd held in his arms was probably four by now, and if anything happened to her because Jackson hadn't moved fast enough…

He shuddered.

"Want me to carry Rex for a while? We're nearly there." Isaac was close on his heels. He'd likely seen Jackson's shiver and mistaken it for fatigue.

"I'm good." Rex was his partner, and he'd see this to the end. "But when we get to the trailhead, I want to take Danica with me to get Everly and Amelia to a safe house. Can you take Rex to see our vet at the training center?" There was a small clinic in the headquarters in Olympia, but it was an hour away and time was crucial. He couldn't be with both his partner and Everly, and Everly was the one he'd been assigned to. Isaac would take good care of Rex and get him the help he needed.

"Anything you need, Jack."

That was Isaac, dependable and a friend, much like everyone else in the K-9 unit. Jackson was grateful for all of them. The members of the team were each assigned to one of the state's national parks, which were spread out across Washington, but if an officer needed backup and a colleague was available, they'd often drive or chopper over to help.

They broke through the trees to the clearing where the parking lot was. Jackson hung back with Everly while Isaac and Freddy made a quick survey of their vehicles, the only four in the lot. When Freddy indicated they were clear of explosives or tracking devices, Isaac motioned them forward.

Jackson spoke to Everly as they reached his SUV, the rain gusting down suddenly. "Is there anything you need from your vehicle? A purse? A backpack? Keys?"

"There's a backpack in the cargo area." She clicked the key fob in her pocket and the crossover's lift gate opened. "Everything's in there, my house keys, and even a change of clothes. It's all stuff I don't like to haul around on the trail, including my wallet. It's probably not the safest place to leave them, but I don't want to risk losing my credit cards or IDs way out there in the middle of nowhere."

She wouldn't need those cards or IDs much longer. Jackson's stomach knotted over what she was about to go through. If she'd truly been found, then Everly Lopez and her daughter were about to vanish without a trace.

Jackson jogged ahead and returned with her backpack, which she slung over her shoulder as he escorted her to his truck. "Get in my vehicle. I'm sending Rex with Isaac and we'll go—"

The back window of the vehicle shattered, and a gunshot retorted through the rain.

Everly screamed and dropped to the gravel.

THREE

Everly screamed again as Jackson dragged her to the side of his SUV and pulled the door open.

He practically lifted her off her feet to shove her into the rear of the vehicle, which appeared to have been converted into a kennel for Rex. He then tossed her backpack in behind her. "Get on the floor and stay down."

Everly dove to the floor and covered her head with her hands. It was like tornado drills in elementary school. The tuck-and-cover position would have done little to protect against a tornado, and it definitely wouldn't stop a bullet. "What about you?"

The SUV rocked as Jackson slammed the door. It was unlikely he'd even heard her question, and he probably wouldn't have answered anyway.

A strange metallic thwack came from the rear of the SUV as another gunshot echoed off the trees that ringed the parking area. More shots followed and Everly curled into a ball, shaking, nauseated and terrified. She hadn't been involved in any of the recent bombings, but this had to be what the witnesses had felt like. Helpless. Frightened. Exposed.

Lord, protect Jackson. Protect Rex. Protect his team.

Get us out of here. Her prayers sounded a lot like the same ones she'd uttered in elementary school during the times those tornado sirens hadn't been drills. Quick, simple and desperate.

Thank God that He heard her no matter how she prayed.

From outside, there were shouts she couldn't understand. One sounded like the female officer with the German shepherd. Danica?

The SUV rocked again as Jackson leaped into the driver's seat and yelled for her to hang on. He started the vehicle and executed a turn in reverse that nearly brought up the energy bars Everly now regretted snacking on earlier. The engine roared as Jackson raced up the gravel road, bouncing into ruts created by the recent rains. He muttered under his breath.

Praying, if she knew him at all.

The car hit another rut, and she grunted as her knees hit her chest.

"Sorry." Jackson slowed, but not much. "I think you can climb up here and buckle in now. I'm taking you somewhere safe. We'll have Isaac and Freddy check the vehicle one more time for bugs, then get you out of here."

He hadn't provided her with much detail about the plans or their destination, likely in case someone was listening.

Everly shuddered as she slipped carefully through a narrow door between the front seats and, maneuvering around equipment, slid into the passenger seat. It wasn't easy, especially with the SUV bouncing along the gravel road.

Neither of them acknowledged how much danger she and Amelia were currently in or how much every muscle in her body ached to get to her daughter. She believed that Jackson's teammates were keeping a close eye on Amelia, but until they were reunited…

She pulled the seat belt across her chest and clicked it into place, forcing herself to focus on the moment.

How had this happened? Giving up her family and her life in Texas was supposed to prevent their ever being found. She'd been careful. Hadn't contacted anyone. Didn't have social media. Hadn't shown up on any websites or news outlets that she knew of. "How was I found?" She looked over in time to meet Jackson's eyes.

"I don't know." Before she could read anything into his grim expression, he turned his attention back to the road. His skin almost looked pale, and the lines creasing his forehead and around his mouth were deep.

For the next ten minutes neither of them spoke. The longer they were quiet, the more Everly's stomach churned. She had to get to Amelia. Had to know her daughter was okay. If she'd been found, then what were the chances someone already knew where her child was? Her eyes slipped shut and she forced herself to breathe deeply, the way her therapist had taught her, fighting down waves of panic. Her arms ached as much as her heart. She wanted to hold her daughter and know she was well.

"Amelia's going to be okay." Jackson's words were soft, barely above a whisper.

He'd been observing her. "How do you know that?" When she opened her eyes, he was watching the road.

"Because Isaac got the call out to the team and they're keeping an eye on the house. Nobody's going to get to Amelia without a military platoon and several tanks. I promise."

The certainty in his eyes soothed her, but only for a moment. She wouldn't calm down until she had her child in her arms.

Not even then, because someone had found them. This wasn't over when she reached Amelia. It was only beginning.

Slowing, Jackson turned onto an overgrown dirt service road and drove deep into the trees before he turned the SUV around in front of a dilapidated wooden shed to face the road.

Another SUV, identical to his and also bearing federal markings, pulled in behind them, leaving his path back to the road clear.

Jackson opened the door and stepped out, barely looking at her. "Stay in the car."

Not on his life. If they were going to talk about her, then she wanted to hear every word. There was no way someone had followed them with the circuitous route Jackson had taken. Not even she was sure where they were, and she knew this section of Olympic National Park as well as she knew her own backyard.

The backyard she would never see again.

Shaking off that thought, she climbed out of the SUV and followed Jackson to where he huddled with the male officer who'd met them on the trail.

Isaac McDane—according to his nameplate— flicked a glance at Everly before turning his attention back to Jackson. "Freddy and I will sweep your vehicle one more time and make double sure there are no bugs, then you guys can get out of here. Tanner will have an unmarked vehicle waiting for you at this rendezvous point with a kennel in the back and a car seat ready to go." He handed Jackson a slip of paper, then tipped his head to acknowledge Everly's presence. Giving a command to his partner, he walked around them to Jackson's SUV.

Jackson turned and noticed Everly. He almost said something but stopped, though his eyes fired a silent warning. There was no doubt in Everly's mind that he knew her well enough to remember her stubborn streak and wouldn't challenge her, at least while they were relatively safe.

Everly wrapped her arms around her stomach, anxious to get to her daughter, but that couldn't happen until the way was cleared. She chewed the inside of her lip for a moment before blurting out the first question that came to her mind. "Where's Rex?"

The line between Jackson's eyes deepened. "When the shooting started, we loaded him in Danica's vehicle because it was the closest. She's on her way to our vet with him now." He tipped his head, letting his eyes drift down to her arms, which were tightening around her stomach more with each passing moment. "How are you holding up?"

"I just want to get to Amelia." Her voice cracked on the pressure of the unshed tears that blocked her throat. A shudder started deep in her stomach and worked its way out to her extremities. Fear, crashing adrenaline and soaking wet clothes created a perfect storm that threatened to rattle her into pieces.

"I know." Jackson stepped closer but stopped when he was still a couple of feet away. "And you're probably freezing."

"So are you." His lips looked almost blue. "I have clothes in that bag you threw into the back seat."

He turned away from her. "Isaac, have Freddy check

her bag, then toss it over here. Grab mine from the cargo area, too, if you don't mind."

Isaac dropped both bags to the ground and had his partner sniff and nudge them. After a thorough inspection, Freddy sat, looking up at Isaac expectantly.

"You're clear." Isaac tossed the bags to Jackson and went back to his search of the vehicle.

After passing her the backpack, Jackson walked around to the side of Isaac's SUV and opened the kennel door. "Climb in and change into your other clothes. I'll go help Isaac, then change in my vehicle."

After he'd shut the door gently behind her, Everly ducked down and slipped into a dry sweatshirt and joggers, feeling slightly better as the soft warmth settled against her skin.

But the comfort on her outside seemed to thaw the ice that had been holding her raging emotions at bay. As her skin warmed, tears slipped down her cheeks. Leaning forward over her knees, Everly laid her head against the back of the front seat and let them fall without wiping them away.

This was it. The day she'd had nightmares about and had lived in fear of for years had finally come. Not only was she separated from her daughter, but their lives were in immediate danger, so close that they'd have to be relocated… If an assassin didn't find them first.

So much was spinning out of control, but one thing was certain. No matter how this nightmare ended, she had no doubt that she was targeted for death.

Jackson watched the mirrors as much as he watched the road in front of him, his fingers cramping from their grip on the steering wheel of the unfamiliar SUV. While several cars had appeared and disappeared behind them since they'd made the vehicle exchange with K-9 Officer Tanner Ford, he hadn't picked up a tail.

That wasn't necessarily a good thing. He'd learned long ago that it wasn't what was seen that caused trouble. Most of the time, it was the unseen that swooped in and attacked.

Like his past feelings for Everly, who now sat in the passenger seat, hidden behind darkly tinted windows.

Those emotions had come out of the blue like the car bomb that killed Lance Carnalle before his testimony.

Jackson shook away the sight of the smoldering vehicle in the hospital parking lot. Shoved aside the remembered stench of smoke and death. If he let his eyes wander to the past, he took his head out of the game and risked Everly's life in the present.

Everly's *and* Amelia's.

With a last quick glance in the rearview, he turned onto the road that led into the neighborhood where Everly's friend Tara was babysitting Amelia. Though the sky had lightened some, the afternoon was still overcast, and the streetlights were lit in the modest middle-class subdivision. Consulting the directions he'd had Everly write down for him, he slowed the SUV a little too quickly, still adjusting to the brakes.

The vehicle was a Park Service backup, slightly different than the large SUVs that were outfitted for everyday K-9 use. His regular vehicle had no back seat. The space was taken up by a kennel with constant air conditioners and alarms that would warn him if the power failed.

This SUV wasn't tricked-out that way. The back seat was intact and, true to his promise, Tanner had made sure a car seat was in place for Amelia. But the kennel space in the cargo area was smaller and had fewer features. He'd have to be careful how he handled things the next few days to make sure Rex was kept safe.

Well, he'd have to be careful once Rex was cleared for duty again. Jackson said another quick prayer for his partner, hoping that Danica would call with an update soon. Kate Waldorf, their veterinarian at HQ, was likely examining Rex right now and would have him up and at 'em fast. *Please, Lord.*

"Tara lives in the last house on the left." For the first time since they'd transferred vehicles at an abandoned fire tower deep in the forest, Everly spoke. Although she'd been silent, the closer they'd gotten to her friend's house, the more she'd shifted in her seat and sat forward against the seat belt, as though she could somehow get to her daughter faster by focusing her energy on what lay ahead.

"Thanks." Jackson slowed as he neared the end of the street, noting the Park Service sedan at a vacant house two doors down and an SUV in the driveway of Tara's home. He'd known that members of his team would be close, but actually seeing them took some of the edge off his stress.

He pulled into the driveway and parked beside the other SUV in a spot close to the front door.

Everly reached for the door.

"Wait." She didn't need to rush out into the open until he got the high sign that all was clear. He scanned the area for one of his teammates and for hidden threats.

Everly waited, although she fidgeted more with each second that passed. Her daughter was so close...

PNK9 Officer Ruby Orton rounded the corner of the

house from the side yard and gave Jackson a thumbs-up as Asher Gilmore came from the other direction and stood near the front door.

"Okay, you can—" The slamming of the door cut off the rest of his sentence as Everly raced around the front of the SUV.

The door of the house burst open, and a little girl in a blue cartoon T-shirt and blue jeans raced out, a dark braid bouncing behind her. She threw herself into her mother's arms, and Everly held on tight, her face buried in the child's hair.

Jackson looked away. The last time he'd seen Amelia, she'd been just a couple of months old, still keeping Everly awake for most of the night.

Now she was four.

Just a year younger than Lance Carnalle's son, who'd just started walking when his father died on Jackson's watch.

He slipped out of the SUV and stood beside it, watching as Asher gently herded Everly and Amelia to the front door.

Everly paused on the steps, turning to look straight at Jackson as if to ask if he was coming inside.

He waved her on. Right now, he couldn't. Too much of his past was swamping his present. Everly's reappearance and danger, the memories of his failure to—

"You're nosediving into that black hole you go into about Carnalle, aren't you?" His colleague Ruby Orton stepped to his side with her black Lab, Pepper, who specialized in search and rescue. As she approached, she reached into her pocket and held out a cell phone. "Before you lie to me about that, take this. Isaac told us your cell took a dive, so Jasmin downloaded your phone innards out of the cloud and loaded them onto a replacement. You're welcome."

As he took the phone, she eyed him before reaching over to brush at something on his shoulder.

Jackson took a step back. Ruby was fastidious about dog hair, and he was likely covered in Rex's even though he'd changed clothes. If he wasn't careful, Ruby would come at him with one of the lint rollers she kept at the ready.

He held up the phone between them. "Thanks." He felt whole again, having contact with the outside world. Sliding the device into his thigh pocket, Jackson leaned against the SUV's hood. "We can't stay long. I need to get Everly and Amelia to a safe house until the WITSEC team arrives. Somebody has to get them clothes and—"

"Way to evade the question about Carnalle, Jack." Her soft Alabama drawl made the observation sound less forceful than she likely meant it to. Ruby didn't pull punches.

She also knew Jackson better than anyone else on the team. Ruby was one of the few who'd drawn the whole story about Carnalle out of him. That made her an ally most of the time…and an irritation some of the time.

He exhaled loudly and gave up his planned defense. Ruby would know he was lying. "That's crossed my mind a few times."

"Because he's the reason you left the Marshals." She tipped her head toward the house. "The reason you left those two behind."

He'd never had to tell Ruby that he'd started feeling… things…for Everly as he'd gotten to know her. That those feelings had only grown when he'd prayed through the postpartum infection that had nearly robbed Amelia of her mother.

Ruby was intuitive. She'd figured it out.

She mimicked his posture, leaning against the truck a few feet away with Pepper at her feet. "I don't know how many times I have to tell you that his death wasn't your fault." She held up a hand when he started to speak. "The Marshals Service has never lost a protected witness who followed the rules. You know this. You aren't the one who messed up."

On paper, that was true. The week before Lance Carnalle was scheduled to testify against cartel leader Geoffrey Korbo, a car bomb had been placed while he was visiting his mother in the hospital, leaving a crater in the parking lot, the prosecution without their star witness, and the Carnalle family without a husband and father. True, Lance had only been testifying to protect himself, but he'd been a human being.

And Jackson had let him die. "I should have had the detail keep a closer eye on him. He'd talked about seeing his mother, and the talk only increased as the date for her surgery approached." He shook his head. "In my gut, I knew he was going to do it. I should have spoken up and I didn't." He'd been distracted by a baby girl and her mother, whom he never should have let into his heart in the first place.

Despite everyone telling him that Carnalle's actions weren't his fault, Jackson had opted for a change, for a job that would allow him to continue protecting the public but would eliminate the kinds of personal distractions that got people killed.

In his current position, he wasn't attached to people but to cases. He investigated and moved on. Sometimes, he offered comfort in the moment, but there was no prolonged contact that could lead to complications.

This was better. It kept him from mistakes.

Deadly mistakes.

"You're one of the most focused officers we have on the team, but you can get a little intense." Ruby leaned down and scratched Pepper behind the ears. "You breathe and probably even sleep this job. There's no way you're totally happy doing that. It might do you good to consider having a personal life."

"I'm perfectly content with my job and my life. If I was ever going to consider going out with anyone, it certainly wouldn't be with a protected witness." As long as Everly was in WITSEC, she'd need to remain vigilant. Whoever made a life with her would also have to be on guard.

That man was not Jackson.

He had long ago buried any growing feelings for her. There was no need to resurrect them now.

It was time to shift the spotlight off himself. "Speaking of personal lives…"

"Were we?" Ruby bent to give Pepper a two-handed belly rub.

Now who was dodging questions?

This ought to take the heat off him. "Willow told me she saw you and Eli Ballard making gooey eyes at each other." Normally Jackson would be happy that Ruby was dating someone. But Eli was the business partner of Stacey Stark, whose murder the PNK9 were currently investigating. Stacey and her boyfriend, Jonas Digby, had been shot to death in Mount Rainier National Park back in April. Eli wasn't a suspect at this time, but the team was keeping tabs on everyone close to the victims.

The team had been thrown into a spin because the prime suspect was their own rookie crime scene investigator, Mara Gilmore. She'd been seen running from the murder scene. She hadn't taken any of the chief's calls, and she was still in hiding. The stress of finding Mara and solving the murders was working on all of them.

"It's nothing serious." But as Ruby gave Pepper a final pat and straightened, she dropped Jackson a sly wink that said otherwise. "Enough about me, let's talk about Rex. I'm sure he'll be just fine."

"I'm sure, too. But there's no reason to be evasive about seeing Eli Ballard. I say good for you." Ruby deserved some joy in her life.

"When have you known me to be evasive about anything? Ever?" She stepped away from the vehicle and kicked his boot. "And…hypocrite much? A relationship is good for me but not for you?"

Had she seriously managed to flip the conversation back to him? "Let it go. I'm not—" In his pocket, his new phone buzzed. *Saved by the literal bell.* Holding up a finger, he drew it out and glanced at the screen.

Donovan Fanelli. He turned the phone so Ruby could see it, then answered. If their chief was calling, it was big news. "Jackson Dean."

"Jack, are you with the witness you were sent to retrieve?"

At the urgency in Donovan's tone, Jackson frowned. "I am."

"Get her to a secure location. Now. They've located Deputy Marshal Anderson." Donovan's tone was tight.

Something was wrong. Had Anderson turned on Everly? Had he been compromised? Jackson was already in motion, striding toward the house with Ruby and Pepper close behind, his gaze sweeping the area as dread built in his gut. "What's wrong?"

"He's dead, Jack. Murdered. His car and body were torched in a remote area of the park."

FOUR

"What kind of trouble are you in, Ev?" Tara grabbed Everly by the arm as soon as she set Amelia on her feet and dragged her into the kitchen, her brown eyes bright with concern. "Is this about the bomber? I thought they caught that guy."

Everly tried to turn back toward the living room where Amelia was playing quietly with Tara's youngest daughter, Casey, but her friend held tightly to her wrist. "You can see her from here. She's fine. And with an entire military guard outside of my house, I don't think you have to worry about anyone busting in." Tara released her and tipped her chin to force Everly to look her in the eye. "Seriously. Are you okay?"

This was one of the things Everly liked best about Tara. She was blunt and to the point. She was a great listening ear, was consistent in praying for her loved ones and didn't let Everly back away from her feelings. The ache of a future without Tara's friendship knotted her chest. There would never be another like her.

But at times like this, there was a fine line to walk. Tara had no idea that Everly was a protected witness. Even though her WITSEC identity now appeared to be blown, the less Tara knew, the better it was for everyone. It would keep her friend safer to remain in the dark. Everly chewed her lower lip, glancing again at her daughter, who was playing in blissful ignorance in the living room where she'd spent countless happy hours.

Everly's eyes drifted shut. They would probably never come back to this warm, welcoming home again. The white shiplap on the walls and the open cabinets were straight from a television show that Tara had obsessed over before doing the work herself, with Everly's help. They'd poured literal sweat and blood into these walls.

Tara and her husband and her children meant so much to her. They were the closest thing Everly and Amelia had to family, since hers was out of reach.

Lord, please don't let me cry now. I can't put Tara and her family in danger by telling them the truth or taking the risk of telling them goodbye. But what exactly could she say?

"Ev? You're starting to scare me more than a bunch of officers showing up at my house with dogs and guns."

"I'm sorry. And it's not about the bombings last month." Even though the perpetrator was in jail, the scars remained. It had been a harrowing few weeks for the people who lived around the park.

Exhaling slowly, Everly opened her eyes and forced herself to focus on her best friend. "I was on the trail today and a man attacked me. It—"

"Everly. No." Tara gripped her biceps and turned her friend to face her. "Are you okay? Did he hurt you?" Her eyes widened as she scanned Everly's face.

"No. I'm fine. He didn't get a hand on me. I'm a crack shot with bear spray." She relayed a brief summary of her escape, glossing over the scariest parts and leaving out the fact that she'd met Jackson before. That would open another line of questioning that she couldn't fully dive into.

"But why all of the personal attention from the PNK9?" Tara was smart enough to pick up the things that Everly wasn't putting down.

She was so tired of lies. Her entire life was nothing but a giant lie. But she couldn't divulge the truth now. Too much was at stake. "The man knew my name. It seems like he personally came after me, and until we know why, the PNK9 team want to know that Amelia and I are safe." That might be skating a bit too close to the truth, but she owed her friend something.

Tara's eyebrows drew together, and she released Everly's arms, walking to the bar that separated the kitchen from the living room to look at the girls, who had moved on to a fierce Star Wars–style battle with foam lightsabers. "Is my family safe? With all of the attention here…"

Jackson had mentioned plans to protect Tara's family on the ride over. "Someone will reach out to you about keeping an eye out here for a day or so, if you want. But once I'm gone, you and the kids and Robert should be fine."

Nodding slowly, Tara turned back to Everly. "What about you? What do you mean by *gone*?"

Everly looked away. The true story? She'd cease to exist. Everly and Amelia Lopez would be absorbed into a government system that eradicated their lives and built new ones from scratch. New home. New friends. New church.

New identity. Her life would be wiped out. All of the work toward her doctorate would vanish. The late nights writing papers and studying research would bear no fruit. Her position with the Department of Fish and Wildlife would disappear. She'd be left with nothing.

Nothing but Amelia.

Her baby girl was enough.

"Everly? You zoned out on me."

Sagging against the stainless steel refrigerator, Everly crossed her arms over the chill in her heart. "I don't know." It was the best she could offer to the woman who had poured so much of herself into Everly's and Amelia's lives.

It didn't feel like enough.

"You're not going home tonight, are you?" Without waiting for an answer, Tara headed for the living room. "Amelia has a few toys here, and she and Casey are the same size. I'll pack up some clothes and a few things to keep her occupied." She vanished down the hallway on the other side of the house.

Everly took a deep breath and tried to grasp what was happening. How could she leave behind a friend like Tara? A church like Grace Chapel? Her job? Her—

The front door opened so quickly it banged against the wall.

Everly jumped.

The loud thump sent Amelia scurrying for her mother as Jackson stepped into the house, his expression tense and dark.

Everly bent and picked up her daughter as she ran into the kitchen, snuggling her close. "It's okay, baby. You're safe with Mama." But was she? Because this was it. This was the moment for goodbyes. Everything about Jackson's expression and posture said so.

Everly couldn't look away from him, and he didn't

speak. He simply stood there looking like he wished he could deliver better news.

Tara's voice came up the hallway ahead of her. "I packed a few things into one of Robert's old backpacks and I added…" Her voice trailed off when she saw Jackson. Her gaze shifted quickly from him to Everly and back again. "You guys are leaving, aren't you?"

Jackson simply offered a curt nod.

Pulling in a deep breath, Everly focused on what she'd been taught in DC on her first go-round. *How do you tear your life apart and rebuild it again? One inhale at a time.*

She walked around the island and hugged Tara with her free arm as Amelia clung tightly to her neck. "Thank you for everything." It wasn't enough, but it would have to do. Maybe she could have the Marshals Service deliver a message to Tara later, explaining as much as possible.

Until then, this was goodbye.

Backing away, Tara gave her a concerned look, her forehead wrinkled with confusion and questions. She passed the backpack to Everly. "You know I love you both, girl. Be safe. And call me when you can." She placed a kiss on the back of Amelia's head and murmured something Everly couldn't hear.

Everly blinked back tears. That phone call would never happen.

Before she could break down, she hustled for the door, pausing to give Casey a quick hug where she stood wearing mismatched clothes that indicated her mother had let her choose today's outfit, and with her lightsaber held limply at her side.

Then, Everly let Jackson usher her out the door and away from her life.

* * *

They were five miles from the house before Everly asked the question he'd been dreading. "What happened to make you rush us out?"

This was the fine line he'd walked when he'd worked with Witness Protection and that he walked now as a law enforcement officer. Did he tell the full truth? Or did he pull punches to protect the victim?

Pulling punches kept the edge off fear, but it also hindered trust when the truth inevitably came to light.

He needed Everly to trust him. Given what she'd already seen and been through because of Kassandra Rennish, she probably already had some clue as to what was happening.

He gripped the steering wheel with both hands and checked to make certain Ruby was still behind him. Backup made him feel less alone and as though Everly and Amelia were safer than with just his two eyes on them.

"Jackson?" Everly cleared her throat and looked away from him out the passenger window as though this would be easier if she couldn't see his face. "How bad is it?"

This time when he checked the rearview, he sought out Amelia in the back seat. She was happily occupied with a book that was making all sorts of noises when she pressed the buttons on the side of it. If he heard one more duck quack...

But at least she wasn't listening to the grown-ups.

Still he kept his voice low. "Deputy Marshal Anderson is..." He hated the word. Didn't want to say it. Didn't want to believe it. He'd only met the man a couple of times, but he was a member of the law enforcement community and he'd been connected to Everly. That made this personal.

Everly breathed in and out slowly, then looked at him. "They killed him trying to find out where we were."

No sense in lying about it. "It looks that way. I don't have details yet."

"So how did they find out…" She shook her head. "You wouldn't know that yet, either."

"How did they find out that Anderson was connected to you?" If only he knew. Information like that was locked down tight. Anything that could lead to the whereabouts of a protected witness was secured. WITSEC had never lost a single person who'd followed the rules. It was unthinkable that the streak would end now, with Everly. "I have no idea."

The silence between them stretched long. She fidgeted with her seat belt, twining it between her fingers. "Now that we're away from Tara's, can you tell me where we're going?"

Everly was smart. She knew Jackson wouldn't be in the picture for long. He was temporary protection, but the Marshals Service would take over for her relocation. "We're meeting a team in Enumclaw. You'll be transferred to them and moved as quickly as possible. I don't know if they'll route you to DC or if they'll educate you about your new identities on the fly. DC is preferable, but given the circumstances with Deputy Marshal Anderson, I don't know." He looked over to her and found her pulling at the hem of her sweatshirt. "I wish I could offer you more."

"And I wish you were coming with us." She offered him a sad smile. "I knew you. Trusted you. You were… a friend."

Something he never should have been. It was dangerous to get emotionally involved. "It's better this way."
What he really wanted to say was that he'd missed her
friendship as well, but this wasn't the time or place.

There would never be a time or place for that.

"I'm sure someone thinks it is." The murmur was almost too low for him to hear. He had no doubt she was
weary with following rules and being overly cautious,
especially now that it had all been for naught.

"I know this is hard, and I wish I had more than
words." He sniffed a bitter chuckle. "I can't even give
you understanding because I've never been in your
shoes. Choosing to uproot your life once is hard. But
having to do it a second time must feel impossible."

Her dry, humorless laugh echoed his. "You have no
idea, but I appreciate that you're trying."

"I aim to please." This time, he really did smile. "I
know this about you, though. You're incredibly strong.
You'll build something amazing out of these ashes. I
have no doubt."

"I held on tight to that verse for the first year we were
here. 'To appoint unto them that mourn in Zion, to give
unto them beauty for ashes, the oil of joy for mourning,
the garment of praise for the spirit of heaviness; that
they might be called trees of righteousness, the planting of the Lord, that he might be glorified.'"

"That's from Isaiah 61."

"You marked it in the Bible you gave to me." Everly
sat taller, squaring her shoulders as though his words
had braced her for whatever was to come. But then she
turned to look into the back seat at her daughter, and
her spine seemed to lose some of its strength. "I understand it, and I'll get through it. I've survived this before,

largely because you helped me set my focus on eternal life more than this life. This is temporary. It's always been temporary. It's just..." The words choked off.

Jackson pulled his eyes from the road long enough to take in her tightly pressed lips and the lines in her forehead. He recognized that expression. She was trying not to cry.

He was pretty sure he knew why. "You can handle it, but Amelia's only four, and you're concerned about how she'll—"

"Amelia! I'm four!" From the back seat, a tiny voice interjected itself into the conversation. Clearly, someone had heard their name.

Everly exhaled through pursed lips and reset her expression before she turned toward her daughter. "Yes, you are. You just turned four. Did you hear Mr. Jack talking about you?"

"Uh-huh."

"Did you hear anything else?"

"Nope." Amelia clipped the word, flashing a smile when she caught Jackson watching her in the rearview. "Mr. Jack, I'm four."

He couldn't help but smile back. When Everly had reintroduced them at Tara's house, Amelia had immediately shortened his name. He rather liked it. "So I hear." It tilted his world to think about how the little girl in the back seat was the same impossibly tiny infant he'd helped to care for when Everly was recovering in the hospital. He'd once been a part of this little stranger's life. The past folded over the present like a blanket, suffocating him.

Apparently, Amelia grew bored with his throwback-to-the-past silence because the back seat started to moo and bark again, indicating she'd gone back to her book.

A few more *moos* passed before Everly spoke, her voice lower than it had been earlier. "You're right. How do you tell a child that she's just lost everything? Even her name?" Tears thickened her words. "We've been working on writing her name and she's so proud of being able to…" With a sniff, Everly turned to stare out the passenger window again. "I just want this to be over. For good."

As long as Kassandra Rennish wielded power—and worse, was out of prison—that would never happen.

Laying his hand on Everly's shoulder, Jackson gave a quick squeeze of support. There was nothing he could do but listen and then turn her over to the team that would whisk her away forever.

His phone chirped through the speakers.

"Hello!" Clearly, Amelia was aware of how Bluetooth worked in vehicles.

Fishing his cell from his pocket, Jackson answered on the device. There was no way he was going to risk putting that call on speaker when he had no idea what the person on the other end might say. He tapped the screen to answer and pressed the phone to his ear. "Jackson Dean."

"Abort the transfer." PNK9 Chief Donovan Fanelli's voice was strained. "Jackson, do not meet the marshals to make the transfer."

Jackson's jaw tensed. He glanced at Everly, who was watching him with concern. "Is there an explanation?" Not handing Everly and Amelia over to WITSEC was a huge derailment in the plan. It meant something had gone horribly, systemically wrong.

Something way bigger than Everly.

"Given the circumstances surrounding Deputy Marshal Anderson's death, our contact is concerned there's a mole and someone might be waiting at the exchange point."

Adrenaline shot white-hot through Jackson. A mole? In the US Marshals Service? The consequences were too monumental to even imagine and could prove deadly for protected witnesses across the country. "Plan?"

"The witness is ours to protect for the near future. I'm making this your assignment and will ensure you have assistance from anyone not actively working our current cases. Get back here to headquarters, and we'll make a plan."

"Understood." He slipped the phone into his pocket after Donovan killed the call, then lifted his foot from the accelerator. He needed to turn around and get back to the highway.

"What's wrong?" Everly laid a hand on his bicep. "I remember you well enough to know that wasn't good news."

It wasn't. But how did he tell her she was in more danger now than ever before?

FIVE

Pain radiated from Everly's shoulders, up her neck and into her throbbing head. She adjusted her posture in the hard plastic chair behind a table in the classroom at PNK9 headquarters in Olympia, but it did little to ease the tension. She'd always carried her emotions in her shoulders. Now was not the time for her to develop a raging headache.

Eating would help, but the package of crackers Jackson had brought to her wasn't appetizing. She'd abandoned them on the table beside a can of soda and a bottle of water.

Instead of eating, she turned a bear spray holster over in her fingers, considering the feel of the brown and orange canvas. What had once been so important was now useless. Yet another thing she'd have to discard along with her identity.

"Mama, look!" At the front of the room, Amelia scribbled on a massive whiteboard miles larger than the laptop-sized board she usually doodled on. Her current obsession was drawing her interpretation of apple trees, which consisted of two parallel lines with a circle on the top and dots for the fruit.

The board was covered in a chaotic orchard of gangly trees.

"That looks nice, baby." She really ought to get out of this chair and focus on her daughter, who was handling the whiplash of the afternoon like a champ. Setting the holster in front of her, Everly shoved out of the chair and rounded the table to search the whiteboard ledge for more markers. If nothing else, she could add to the growing apple orchard on the board. "If I had another marker, I'd draw with you."

"I'll share." Amelia offered her the single black marker. "All of my apples are black, though."

"Then they can be anything you want them to be. Apples, pears—"

Two taps sounded on the door to the hallway, and the tall female officer Jackson had been talking to earlier stepped into the room, holding a fistful of colorful dry erase markers. Her dark hair hung to her shoulders, and her brown eyes sparkled. She smiled with a sheepish grin. "I overheard there was only one marker and no colors, so I ducked across the hall and grabbed some from the other room."

Amelia bounced on the balls of her feet, her braid swinging with the motion. "Thank you, Miss—" She planted her hands on her hips. "What's your name?"

The officer crouched and held out the markers. "I'm Ruby. And these are for you."

"Ruby is a princess's name." Amelia tapped the officer on the nose with the black marker.

Drawing back with a smile, Ruby stood. "I figure if you use yellow, you can make a lemon tree. Orange makes an orange tree." Her Southern drawl was pronounced, adding warmth to her voice.

Amelia lunged for the woman, grabbing a purple marker and popping the cap off before attacking the closest "tree" on the board. "And purple for a grape tree!"

Catching Ruby's quick glance, Everly bit down on a chuckle. Neither of them corrected her daughter about plant biology. Let her kiddo draw all of the "grape trees" she wanted. The activity was keeping her occupied and happy.

Everly slid onto the table while Ruby chatted with Amelia. She surveyed the room they'd been waiting in for over fifteen minutes. It was sterile, definitely a government institution. The walls were white, broken up by windows that looked out over a fenced yard where the dogs were clearly trained. White tables and brown plastic chairs sat on top of oatmeal-colored tile. A few posters of dogs and gear were scattered around the room, but there was no decoration otherwise.

It felt like every college classroom she'd ever sat in. Reaching behind her, Everly grabbed the holster and ran her finger down the stitching. Everything was moving so fast. Her brain couldn't keep up.

"What's that?" Ruby leaned against the table beside her and reached over to tap the orange canvas. She leaned closer. "Looks like a bear spray holster."

"It is."

"I like it. The ones we carry are plain black. That one's got personality. Where'd you find it?"

"It was given to me."

"So, it has a story?"

"Nothing very exciting." But still, with all of the emotions raging like a volcano in her stomach, it might help to let some of the steam out. Everly lifted a half smile. "At orientation when I started my internship with Fish and Wildlife, we were issued bear spray and the obligatory black holsters." She leaned to the side and pointed to the one on Ruby's belt. "Just like that."

Ruby thunked hers with her index finger. "Ugly as sin, aren't they?"

"One of the girls thought so. Her name was Felicity. She came in the next day with one of these for everybody. They aren't standard-issue, but we were allowed to keep them. She said, 'We need some color in our lives. Even if it's orange.'" The memory drew a larger smile. "Felicity didn't last long out in the field. She liked her air-conditioning and her manicure. But she was so much fun to be around. What you saw was what you got." Something that hadn't been true about Everly in years.

Silence reigned for several minutes, save for the thud of the marker point against the board as Amelia enthusiastically pressed purple dots all over her trees. Those markers wouldn't last five minutes, just like the ones at home, may they all rest in peace.

"It's not easy." Ruby's voice was almost a whisper. "Jackson filled me in a little bit on your situation, but it's staying close to the vest, with only a handful of us in the PNK9 getting all of the details." Ruby sighed. "It's tough to leave everything behind and start over."

Everly tilted her head. *Hang on.* "That almost sounded like you understood, like there's a story there." Yeah, she had no problem being nosy if it would get her head out of her own situation for a minute.

It almost looked like the other woman startled, but she recovered and raised her eyebrows in amusement. "Oh, see? You should leave the reading between the lines to those of us who are trained to investigate." Ruby kicked her booted foot against Everly's. "So, whatever happened to Felicity who liked her comfort?"

So, it was going to be like that. No deflecting with Ruby. In a different world, the two of them could have been friends. "Felicity switched to an internship position in an air-conditioned office, sifting through the data that field researchers like me bring in. We get coffee together a couple of times a month." Reality stole her smile. "Well, we did."

Everly turned to stare out the window at the darkening sky. She was in her last semester of grad school. Ready to defend her dissertation on the effects of tourism and industry on the black bear population. Now what? She couldn't go back to being a veterinarian like she had been in Texas. Couldn't use her knowledge of Pacific Northwest wildlife and habitats to get a job anywhere. She couldn't keep any ties to her old life.

She couldn't even go to her house to retrieve anything. The Marshals would do that. The only object she had that identified her as Everly Lopez was the canvas holster in her hand.

It would be useless in her new life. The only thing it was good for now was tipping someone off to her former occupation and interests.

She squeezed her fingers tightly around the canvas until the seams dug into her palm. It was time to let go. "Thanks for bringing the markers to my daughter and for giving me a few minutes to process this all in relative silence."

Ruby smiled gently. "So, you figured out what I was doing."

"You aren't that slick." Everly held the holster out to Ruby. "Here. Have a little bit of color in your life."

Reaching for the holster, Ruby hesitated. "Are you sure?"

"I'm sure. You can start a trend in the PNK9. I hear they come in multiple colors."

Ruby chuckled and took the canvas case almost reverently. "Thanks. If you really—"

"Mama!"

Jerked out of the conversation, Everly turned to the board where Amelia had drawn a stick figure with brown lines sprouting in all directions on top and scribbles on the face. Was that supposed to be hair? "Who's that, baby?"

"Mr. Jack. He's going to pick the grapes and give them to me because he's tall and I'm not."

Ruby laughed.

All righty, then. Clearly her daughter was fascinated with "Mr. Jack." It wasn't hard to see why. He exuded a confidence and bravery that made a woman—and clearly a little girl—feel safe and protected.

Given the care he'd given to Amelia during her first couple of weeks of life, it was also possible some part of her daughter remembered his gentle kindness.

If only he would come back into the room. He'd vanished as soon as he'd tucked her away here, leaving Ruby to stand guard in the hallway.

Almost on cue, the door swung open and Jackson strode in. "I heard my name and something about picking grapes." The smile on his face was too wide, and it didn't reach his eyes.

But God love him, he was trying for Amelia's sake.

"Mr. Jack!" Amelia ran to him and threw her arms

around his knees as though he was her long-lost best friend. "I drew you!" She raced back to the board and jabbed a finger against it, smearing one of the arms on the stick figure.

Jackson shot a pointed look at Ruby, then glanced at the door.

With a nod, Ruby hopped off the table, then turned and squeezed Everly's hand. She started to speak, but then turned and walked out, closing the door behind her.

Jackson watched with an arched eyebrow, then looked down at Amelia. "You drew me, huh?" He walked to the board and knelt to eye the artwork close up, as though it was the most important thing in his world. "That looks a lot like me, although I should probably have a long talk with my barber about the hair." He tousled the top of Amelia's head.

Giggling, Amelia ducked away from him. "I'll draw me next." She went back to work, taking her time crafting a figure standing next to "Mr. Jack."

Jackson straightened and walked over to lean against the table beside Everly. "I'd like to talk to you with some of my team present but without Amelia. Given the circumstances, would you be okay with her being out of your sight for a bit? Ruby is a fantastic bodyguard. She can walk Amelia up the hall and out to the kennels to see the dogs. They'll be safe on the property."

The breath in Everly's lungs turned to icy vapor. The last thing she wanted was Amelia out of her sight, but she also didn't want her daughter to overhear anything upsetting when her world was about to be thrown sideways. Amelia deserved stability and peace for as long as possible. "Okay." She gave a tight nod, shocked the word managed to squeeze out of her tear-swollen throat.

Jackson took her hand and squeezed, but he dropped it as quickly as he'd picked it up. Without looking at her, he clapped his hands together. "Amelia. How would you like to see some dogs?"

The purple marker clattered to the whiteboard ledge. "Puppies?"

Jackson's face briefly clouded, but he quickly covered it with a smile. Everly wondered what that was about. "No puppies. Just grown-ups. But would you like to visit them?"

"Yes!" Amelia shouted and took his hand, following him out the door without even a glance back at her mother.

As soon as the door closed behind them, Everly let her chin fall to her chest. The room felt colder, but was it because Amelia had left? Or because Jackson was gone?

Jackson watched Ruby and Amelia disappear up the hallway in the direction of the door to the kennels, then leaned against the cinder block wall next to the classroom. He should go back inside and keep Everly from being alone with her thoughts and what had to be some wildly twisting emotions, but he needed a minute to himself.

There was something happening around his heart. Something that couldn't continue. When he'd first peeked through the window into the classroom, watching Everly chat with Ruby, the pain on her face had been a knifepoint against his heart.

But Amelia drawing his picture on the board had driven the knife straight in and left him bleeding. That girl had wrapped him around her little finger in the hospital NICU, when he'd been on deck with her. He'd managed to bury that affection, but it was roaring back now. She had been so small and helpless and in need of protection. In so many ways, she still was.

But it was her mother who twisted the knife in his chest. When he'd touched her hand, all he'd wanted was to prolong the grasp. To put his arm around her and pull her against him to comfort her.

To comfort her as a friend. That was all this was. They'd been friends once, and that was further than it ever should have gone in the first place. But their situation had been unique, and their friendship had been special.

He'd missed their relationship. Had missed her. And now, once she was safely with the Marshals, he'd have to let her go again. It might be harder this time than the last—

"Jackson." His name rang up the hallway. Chief Donovan Fanelli leaned out his office door. His broad shoulders seemed to fill the frame. "We're ready."

He glanced at the classroom door again. Did he dare leave Everly totally alone?

The chief waved him closer and, as Jackson approached, Donovan lowered his voice, his blue eyes intense. "She'll be fine. Nobody is going to get to her in this building. Besides, she probably needs a few minutes alone anyway. She's got a lot to process, and mothers don't typically do that in front of their children."

With a last look up the hall, Jackson followed the older man across the hall. "You may be right. Everly was always the type that had to retreat in order to cope."

"So, you're calling her by her first name?" Donovan's eyebrow arched as he pulled open the door and gestured for Jackson to enter ahead of him.

"We have a history. I was with her when she made her move from DC into WITSEC and when she had her daughter in the hospital. It's a long story." He ended there as he stepped into the room. A large chunk of the K-9 Unit was already gathered at the long tables, which formed a rectangle in the room. Clearly, they either had a new case or they had news on one of their ongoing investigations. Surely they weren't going to let this many people in on the true story about Everly and Amelia. That would be too many people involved with an issue that needed to remain quiet for as long as possible.

Isaac looked up from his spot about halfway down the table near the window. "How's Rex?"

Several others murmured support.

Jackson slid into the nearest chair and laced his hands in front of him. "Kate had him transported here here via chopper from the clinic at Olympic National Park. I stopped into the training center a little while ago to see him. He's starting to wake up, but it's going to take some time for him to fully come out of it. Fortunately, the dart didn't puncture deep enough to dump a full dose of tranquilizer into his system. He should be cleared tomorrow afternoon for pickup, but he can't work until the day after at the earliest."

That was a wrench in his plans. If he was in hiding with Everly, how was he going to get back to his partner? Did they dare wait nearly twenty-four hours before moving Everly out of the building? Kassandra Rennish was smart. She'd built a massive organization that had trafficked people across North and South America.

Everly's husband had discovered her treachery and had been gathering evidence when Kassandra murdered him. Everly's testimony as an eyewitness to the killing had led to Kassandra's imprisonment and the demise of her empire.

Her intelligence meant she'd quickly figure out where Everly and Amelia were hiding and would set up surveillance at the building. Moving was a time-sensitive issue.

"Glad to hear it." Officer Tanner Ford relaxed a bit in his chair. "We got the quick version of him being hit, but not the whole story."

"And you won't get the whole story now, either." The chief took a position at the head of the table but remained standing, leaning forward on his palms. "I've got Jackson and Rex assigned to a particularly sensitive case. We'll loop a few of you in, but I need the rest of you to go on as usual. If necessary, we'll fill more of you in on a need-to-know basis."

Murmurs of assent wound around the tables. This was a group used to the need for discretion and to individual assignments. It happened more often than they wished, if they were being honest.

The chief sniffed and straightened. "I called in those of you who were available to give you an update on our missing bloodhounds."

Everyone at the table leaned in. The PNK9 operated on a grant from the federal government, funded by billionaire Roland Evans, whose wife was murdered during a botched mugging in one of the parks. Recently, he'd donated three bloodhound puppies who were good candidates for K-9 training. But two weeks earlier, someone had managed to breach the training center and incapacitate one of the employees, taking the pups and leaving little evidence behind.

Officer Willow Bates was the first to speak. "Have we found them?"

"Not yet, but we're getting closer."

The room seemed to deflate, but the chief held up his hand to indicate he wasn't finished yet. "We received an anonymous tip about an hour ago. According to the tipster, a backyard breeder has the dogs."

"Wait." Officer Asher Gilmore raised a hand. He'd been fidgeting and seemed distracted, but he'd honed in now. Asher was the half brother of their rookie CSI team member Mara Gilmore, who'd gone into hiding after fleeing from the murder scene of her ex-boyfriend and his new girlfriend. It was no wonder Asher was distracted. "We've got several people on our radar for backyard breeding. Horrible conditions. Not taking care of the dogs. Solely using them for profit."

"We're going after one of them." The chief's expression was determined. When he looked like that, things were about to get serious. "Sarge and I, along with Ruby and her K-9, Pepper, are going to head out with Peyton to investigate the tip. We'll be putting together a plan after this meeting."

There was no doubt Peyton Burns had forced herself onto this mission. As the head trainer for the PNK9, she considered herself responsible for what had happened to the pups.

Jackson bit back a complaint. He'd hoped to keep Ruby on his team protecting Everly and Amelia, but he wasn't about to question or contradict Chief Fanelli. Peyton and Ruby worked well together, though, and she'd be an asset to the mission.

He surveyed the assembled officers, sorting through who would be best to help guard Everly and Amelia until WITSEC was cleared. He trusted everyone at the tables, but some were already assigned to other cases. A couple of the officers lived and worked more than three hours away at North Cascades National Park and would need to get back soon, and one in particular, Asher, seemed focused on finding his sister, who could be anywhere at this point. Although Mara hadn't been seen since she'd run from the crime scene in Mount Rainier National Park back in April, she'd sent a text message from a burner phone to Officer Willow Bates, a close friend of hers who believed in Mara's innocence.

As the chief wrapped up the meeting, Jackson tuned back into the conversation, which involved peripheral details about the mission to check out the breeder.

"If you aren't actively working a case or assigned to work with Jackson," the chief said, "I need you to stay close to your phone in case we need you to come in. Is there anything else before we move on?"

"I've got something." Asher spoke up but then he clamped his mouth shut. The way he tapped his index finger on his phone, which rested facedown on the table in front of him, belied a nervousness he didn't typically display. Something was up.

"Go ahead." The chief leaned against the front table, waiting.

"About half an hour ago I got a text." Asher flipped his phone over and drew it closer, pressing the screen so it lit up in front of him. "It was from Mara."

There was a collective intake of air. Not exactly a gasp. More of an expectation.

Before anyone could speak, he looked up from the phone. "I let Jasmin know, and she's already on it."

Their tech expert, Jasmin Eastwood, was as tenacious as one of their tracking dogs on a scent. If that text could be traced, she'd find it.

"Okay." The chief had straightened and stepped closer to the group. "Is it something you can share with all of us or does it need to be kept close?"

"It's nothing we wouldn't expect." Asher picked up the phone and keyed in his passcode. "It says, 'I didn't kill Jonas and Stacey. I can't say more. Dad's life depends on it. And so does yours. I'm sorry.'" He looked up. "That's it."

"Cryptic." The word slipped out before Jackson could stop it. He didn't know Mara as well as Willow or Asher did, and he had serious doubts about her professed innocence. The evidence against Mara was compelling.

Asher shot him a hard look.

The chief turned to Willow. "Have you heard anything from her recently?"

"Nothing." Willow shook her head, then picked up her phone and checked it as though she wanted to be certain. "But what does she mean when she says her dad's life depends on it and Asher's does, too? It sounds like she's being threatened."

"Or she's covering herself." Officer Colt Maxwell said what most of them were thinking.

"Innocent until proven guilty." Willow spat the words.

Asher remained silent. His relationship with their father was strained. The older man had dementia and was in a care home but, to Jackson's knowledge, Asher hadn't seen him in years, still bearing the burden of a past Jackson knew little about. He'd spoken with Asher about forgiveness, but Asher wasn't there yet.

This entire situation had to be brutal for him.

Still, Jackson had to agree with Colt. "It's been three

months. If she was being threatened, why not let us know? Why hide?"

"Maybe she knows the real killer's identity, and their goal is to keep her quiet," Willow offered. She was ever loyal to her friend.

"As skeptical as I am—" Isaac leaned forward "—I know what it's like to be threatened. It's intimidating. Makes you react instead of responding."

The chief held up both hands. "Nothing we say here is going to make a difference to the facts. We'll let Jasmin do her job and trace the text. Asher, you and I will talk when I get back, and we'll puzzle out how you and your father are involved."

Asher muttered under his breath. Probably something about the use of the word *father*.

Ignoring him, the chief turned to Jackson. "Let's put your team together and get moving."

It was clear what Donovan wasn't saying as he rushed the meeting to a conclusion. They needed to light a fire under this operation before someone figured out Everly and Amelia were here, making them easy targets.

SIX

Prayer was harder today than it had ever been.

Everly crossed her arms on the table and rested her forehead on them. She tried to be still and quiet, to let the peace she knew existed soothe her racing thoughts and her swirling emotions.

Instead of calm, she was swamped by a hurricane spinning faster by the second. Not gales of fear. Not deluges of doubt.

Anger.

Anger raged through her soul with the speed of a rain-swollen river, wiping out any peace that dared to step into its path.

She balled her fists. *God, I asked You. Every single day, I asked You. Begged You. For help. For protection. To not let this happen. But here we are. My baby isn't safe. I'm not safe. Even Jackson isn't safe because he's helping us. How could You let me down like this? No warning. No nothing. Just...destruction.*

Beyond the tirade, she didn't want to talk to Him. She'd come to Him faithfully. Had thanked Him and praised Him and submitted her life to Him. Instead of safety in His arms, she'd been literally set adrift in a rising flood.

She reached forward and slammed her fist onto the desk.

"Hey, now." Jackson's voice broke through the blackness behind her closed eyes and in her heart. "Those are government-issued tables. It's a lowest-bidder situation. I'm not sure how much abuse they can take."

Everly sat straight back in the chair, leaving her arms flat on the table, her heart pounding at the sudden intrusion. "You scared me." The words were as fiery as the ones she'd just been silently screaming.

From the doorway, Jackson held up both hands, palms out. "I'm sorry." He walked over and crouched on the other side of the table, looking up at her. "And I understand. This is all…beyond scary."

"It's infuriating." Everly pounded both fists on the table.

Jackson didn't flinch. "I get that, too."

"God blew it, Jackson. Whatever is happening, this wasn't supposed to be it. This is mean. And cruel. And…" The tears she'd been holding back welled in her eyes. "It's wrong." She wrinkled her nose against the sting. "I probably shouldn't talk about God like that, but it's true."

Puffing out air, Jackson laid his hands on her fists. "Right now, that's how you feel. Everything is a mess. It's out of control. We're not going to talk theology or right and wrong or Who God really is. You're feeling things. Don't bottle that up. Tell Him all about it, because that's what a relationship is. I'm pretty sure He's big enough to take it."

Everly pulled her hands from his and shoved away from the table, pacing to the window above the courtyard where Ruby and Amelia were tossing a ball for

Ruby's K-9 partner. Her daughter looked so happy and carefree. To her, this was all a great big adventure, a break in her routine. She had no idea…

If Everly was less of a woman, she'd put her fist through the window.

But, no. Even in the midst of Noah's murder and Kassandra's threats, she'd never been violent.

She'd also never been this angry. "I don't know what to do." Her chin dropped to her chest and the tears came. This time, she didn't try to stop them.

Something rustled behind her, and then Jackson touched her shoulder, turning her gently toward him. He folded her into his arms, her cheek against his chest, and let her sob out her anger and fear and ten thousand other emotions that refused to remain inside any longer.

He simply held her, his chin on the top of her head. He was probably praying for her, too.

It had been forever since someone held her like this. Prayed over her. In fact, the last person to do so had been Jackson, not long before he left, when he'd escorted her into her new home and held her and Amelia to him as he prayed for their protection and peace.

She'd forgotten how tall he was.

How, in that long-ago moment, she'd felt safe.

Like now.

As her tension eased with the release of tears, she let herself rest in this temporary calm.

"I'll tell you what." Jackson eased her away from him and rested his hands on her shoulders, dipping his chin to meet her tear-filled eyes. "You may not know what to do, but I know. How about you let me handle whatever comes our way, and you just love on Amelia and trust me, one minute at a time."

From experience, she knew she was supposed to trust God that way, but right now she couldn't. He seemed to be absent.

But Jackson was here. And the idea of letting him worry about the details did bring her a measure of peace she hadn't felt in what seemed like years. She backed away, letting his hands fall from her shoulders. "One minute at a time."

In this minute, she was safe. She glanced back at her daughter and Ruby. Amelia was safe. She wouldn't think past that.

Swiping her hands under her eyes, she took a tissue Jackson handed her from a box on one of the desks. She winced at the spot on Jackson's shirt where her tears had darkened the green. "Sorry I soaked you."

"No worries at all." He grinned, then jerked his thumb toward the door. "Are you up to heading to the conference room? I want you to meet a couple of people who you may see around, so at least you'll recognize them."

To be honest, she wasn't, but there was no choice. From experience she knew the longer they stayed in a known place the greater the odds of being found. "Okay." She cast one last look out the window. "Is Ruby coming?" She liked the female officer. Though they'd only spoken for a moment, the woman had felt like a blessing.

If God was actually into blessing her.

"No."

It felt like a blow and proof God didn't care what she needed.

"Ruby was assigned to another case. We have some missing pups who were in training to be K-9s. She's going with the chief and our head trainer to follow up on a lead. I've requested her help if they get back while we're still in the middle of this."

The middle of this. Technically, this was all just getting started, and there was no way to know where the middle really was. Once the Marshals determined how she'd been found, they'd take over, and she'd be on the move.

Jackson's presence was only temporary. Soon, everything would be new faces and new places yet again. The fact jolted her stomach in a way no roller coaster ever had.

Everly looked at the floor and took a deep breath. *One minute at a time.* He was here now. "Okay." Something he'd said snagged on her heart. "You guys have missing puppies?" Now she understood why he'd seemed troubled earlier when Amelia had asked about seeing puppies.

He walked over to stand beside her at the window. "Well, they're the equivalent of teenagers now, so not technically puppies. It's three bloodhounds. They were just about the right age to start training, and someone grabbed them out of the exercise yard."

Everly's eyes went straight to Amelia. Someone had stolen puppies from that very spot? They could easily get to her daughter.

Jackson must have sensed her thoughts. "Not the courtyard. The training yard backs up to an open area on the far side of the kennels. There's a fence, but someone cut through it. It's been repaired and is now more secure. Nobody's getting in that way again. You and Amelia are fine."

"And Rex?" She should have asked earlier, but she'd

been wrapped up in her own mess and hadn't considered he had worries outside of her own. "Have you seen him?"

He lifted a small smile and continued watching Ruby and Amelia.

Was there something between him and the female K-9 officer? They seemed close…

Just as quickly, he turned to Everly. "I was with Rex just before I last saw you. He's coming around. Our vet says he should be fine, and I can probably pick him up tomorrow. If we're deep in the middle of nowhere, someone will bring him to me."

"You miss him, don't you?" It was obvious in the restlessness about him, almost as though he'd mislaid something and was searching for it.

"It's kind of like having your right arm removed and stashed somewhere. He's with me almost all of the time, so not having him here is a little odd."

"Even at home?"

"Yep. He even has a bed in my office here. The only time we're apart is when I'm here in meetings or when he's in the kennel. He gets some downtime, and the vets and trainers get to check him out." He tapped his knuckles on the table and looked her full in the eye. "So… conference room? We'll get you introduced to the team and then get on the road."

Everly nodded. "It's probably good to have Amelia outside. I need to explain a few things to her before we overwhelm her with a ton of new people."

Jackson rounded the table and headed for the door. "It's only two new people, but I get your point. I'm guessing you'll have a lot of explaining to do in the next few days."

As she let him usher her toward the door, Everly tried to piece together what she would say to her daughter, how she would explain they could never return home.

They were words she'd thought of many times, but having to actually say them was nothing short of a nightmare.

Jackson reached for the door handle, but Ruby burst through with Amelia on her hip. Her dark skin held a thin sheen of sweat, as though she'd run with Amelia in her arms.

Everly felt her heart rate accelerate. Something had happened. Rushing forward, she took Amelia from Ruby and held her close. *She's safe. In this minute, she's safe.*

After a brief glance at Everly, Ruby addressed Jackson. "I'll stay here with them. The chief needs you in the conference room."

Without looking back, Jackson left the room on the run.

Jackson burst into the conference room where the rest of the team was still gathered and waiting for Everly. "What's going on?"

The chief stepped up as the other officers stood, ready for action.

Their technical expert, Jasmin Eastwood, approached. She'd arrived in the five minutes he'd been out of the room. Her expression was dark. "I was keeping an eye on the monitors for the exterior cameras, and I noticed this." Holding out a large tablet, Jasmin pressed the screen and the device lit up, showing the view from four of the cameras around the building. At all four—the alley to one side, the street out front, the training center in the rear, and the road beside HQ—a vehicle waited with some-one inside.

It was tough to see how many were in each, but two things were clear: Everly and Amelia had been found, and Kassandra Rennish had help.

Jackson bit back words he never said. He'd hoped to get Everly and Amelia out before Rennish realized they were here, but he'd failed. He never should have come to HQ.

The chief exhaled loudly. "Well, that's four we can see. Who knows how many we can't see." He scrubbed his hand along his chin, slipping into planning mode. "The trick is going to be getting Jackson's people out without them picking up a tail."

Officer Colt Maxwell leaned into the circle clustered around the table. "Can we be read in on who Jackson's protecting?"

Jackson had asked Isaac and Danica to be his main backup, since they were already heavily involved, but the rest of the team was largely in the dark. Danica had readily agreed. Having recently rescued her future stepson from a kidnapper, she had a renewed soft spot for children.

"No." The chief's answer was clipped. "The fewer who know, the better. For now, all you need to be aware of is we have a threat outside our doors. Given our location, we need to ensure we don't wind up in a shoot-out in the middle of the street."

With the Pacific Northwest K-9 Unit situated on a street corner in Olympia, that was a concern they considered daily.

"Confrontation or decoys?" Isaac joined the group. Dropping his hand to the table beside him, the chief drummed his fingers, the noise loud in the silence. Donovan Fanelli had a fast-paced, tactical mind and was renowned for thinking on his feet.

His team watched, waiting.

Less than a minute passed. "Here's what we do. We'll call in the local police to help us out, but we'll have to get on the move before they get here. Jackson, you've already pulled Isaac and Danica to go with you since they're already involved. You, Isaac and Danica get loaded into your vehicles, ready to move on our signal. Jackson, they may know your backup vehicle, so we'll send you out in an unmarked full-sized K-9 shop." As Danica and Isaac joined Jackson, the chief addressed the rest of the room. "The rest of you... We can't arrest anyone given no one is breaking laws, but we can question them on the grounds they appear to be surveilling a government building. That will give the rest of us time to pull out one by one. Get together on your way to the garage and decide on routes so you all move differently. Jackson, grab your team and decide on a rendezvous point so you can space out and make sure no one is trailing you. Any questions?"

It wasn't the first time they'd had to create a diversion or evade, so everyone moved for the door.

"Wait." Jackson held up a hand. "I know this seems counterproductive, but I'd like to keep the witness as out of the loop as long as possible." She'd been through enough already. Panicking her would only make everything worse.

He'd simply have to think of a way to explain away Ruby's earlier urgency.

For a second, it looked as though the chief was going to argue, but then he nodded. "Stay tuned in to your earpieces. And those of you confronting, stay safe. We can see four vehicles, but we have no idea how many are actually out there."

That was the scary part.

Jackson stepped into the hall with Isaac and Danica on his heels. When they were clear of the door, he turned to them. "You guys go on down to get your partners and head to the garage. If you'd move the stuff to my new vehicle and be sure Amelia's car seat is ready to go, we can be ready to roll."

The two headed up the hallway toward the back exit, leaving Jackson to figure out what to say to Everly while he made the fifteen-second walk up the hall. The last thing he wanted to do was frighten her, but he did need to get her to move with some urgency.

At the door, he wrapped his fingers around the handle, forced himself to breathe normally, and said a quick prayer for safety and wisdom. It was going to take God, Who was more in charge than Jackson ever could be, to get them out of this one.

As he entered, Everly rushed forward, still holding Amelia. "What are we doing next?" She kept her voice light for Amelia's sake, but there was fear in her eyes.

Without looking at Ruby, who was standing near the window, he gave Everly a small smile. "Given it's almost dark, the chief felt it was best to go ahead and move before we totally run out of light. They're also switching me back to a standard K-9 SUV so Rex will be safe when we get him tomorrow. Danica and Isaac are downstairs now, moving everything to the new vehicle."

Behind her, Ruby nodded her approval of the plan, though she remained tight-lipped.

"Why the urgency?" The suspicion in Everly's eyes was strong. She was smart enough to know he wasn't telling the whole truth. "Ruby rushed in here like something was chasing her."

With a shrug, Ruby managed to look sheepish. "When the chief calls, you answer."

Thanking God for quick-thinking teammates, Jackson nodded. "And he's called us to move, so we need to do just that."

Still looking doubtful, Everly allowed him to usher her into the hall. When Ruby approached, he pointedly met her eyes, then looked at the conference room. Jasmin would brief her.

Ruby answered with a quick squeeze to his arm as he exited the room.

Ahead of him, Amelia bounced in her mother's arms and looked at him over Everly's shoulder. "Where are we going now? Mama says we're on a 'venture." She wriggled so much she nearly slipped out of Everly's arms. "Will there be more doggies?"

"My partner, Rex, will be with us tomorrow." Jackson forced a smile. "Tonight, we're going to go camping."

"Like in a tent?" Her shout was shrill with excitement, and Everly's shoulders hunched as she looked over her shoulder at Jackson with a wince of pain.

That almost made his smile real. "No, like in a cabin. I know a place out in the woods where we can see a whole lot of really cool animals and look at more stars than you've ever seen."

"Can we make s'mores?"

Stepping around Everly, Jackson shoved open the door to the stairwell and motioned for her to walk through, letting his gaze skip past her as she tried to lock eyes with him. She still didn't believe him.

He answered Amelia instead. "Not tonight, because it will be late when we get there. But if we stay an extra night we can." He'd make sure to put chocolate, graham crackers and marshmallows on the list of supplies he was putting together for whoever brought Rex to them.

If only he knew how many nights they had.

His earpiece crackled to life with Colt's voice. "Pulled out two minutes ago heading south. No tail so far."

"Going west. Same." The male voice was so quick that Jackson wasn't quite certain who it was, but it didn't matter. His team was on the lookout.

By the time they reached the garage, two reported tails were called in, but both involved the cars caught on camera surveilling HQ, which had pulled out before anyone could question them.

As he watched Everly buckle Amelia into her car seat, he glanced at Danica and Isaac, who sat waiting in their SUVs, stone-faced and ready to roll. *Lord, keep all of us safe.*

It was the only prayer he had time for. As Everly climbed into the back seat beside Amelia and shut the door, he rounded the vehicle and slid into the driver's seat.

Asher's voice came through the earpiece as Jackson started the SUV. "Headed north. No tail."

That was a good sign. Jackson's eyebrow inched upward.

"You're sure?" The chief's voice cut in.

There was a pause as Jackson watched Danica head for the garage exit. She'd lead out, then fall into line behind Jackson once they were out of town, to help Isaac watch for anyone suspicious who might be trailing.

Asher finally spoke again. "I'm sure."

Either Rennish's crew was on to them or they were short on manpower. This could work out after all.

Jackson coasted to the exit, giving Danica a head start. She radioed in. "On the route. No tail."

"You ready to hit the road?" Jackson finally dared to speak to Everly, glancing at her in the rearview.

"Yes." She held his gaze in the reflection. "Are you sure everything's okay?"

Turning his attention to the exit, he offered her all he dared to give. "As okay as it can be, given the circumstances. Just try to stay out of sight." The darkly tinted rear windows would help. Hopefully no one would get a good view through the windshield into the back seat.

He pulled onto the street and headed onto the predetermined route. Before he'd gone two blocks, a green sedan merged into traffic behind him.

It was one of the cars from the security footage. Somehow, they'd slipped the group who was headed out to question them.

Jackson gripped the wheel tighter as the vehicle mimicked his lane changes. "Isaac?" He needed to say as little as possible if he wanted to keep Everly in the dark.

"I see him." The pause stretched longer than Jackson would have liked. "I'll maneuver him out of the way before you get on the highway. Last thing we need is for them to know which direction you take. It will narrow their search area."

A new voice joined the discussion. "I'm in my personal vehicle." Jasmin had entered the conversation and, clearly, the operation. "My Tesla doesn't look like a government vehicle. If I disrupt them, they're less likely to think they found the right vehicle than if one of our big ol' clearly marked monsters cuts them off."

She was right.

And he was grateful. "Thanks, Jas."

"I'll bring up the rear in case things get ugly," Isaac added. "Let's do this."

The green sedan wove along the street, drawing closer, probably trying to get a better look inside of Jackson's SUV. When it was about two car lengths back, a white Tesla appeared, weaving in and out of traffic. It squeezed in ahead of the green sedan as Jackson reached a yellow light.

Jasmin slammed on the brakes, stopping at the light and effectively keeping the driver of the green sedan from following.

Jackson sped up as much as he dared, made two more rights and jumped on the highway.

"I took off real slow. He's off your scent." Jasmin's voice held an edge. "You guys are safe."

For now. Jackson dared to peek at Everly, who was watching the cars on the highway. He had no doubt danger would find them again.

SEVEN

It was full dark by the time Jackson reached the end of the winding dirt road to the Park Service cabin in Olympic National Park, not far from where their whole adventure had started.

Isaac and Freddy trailed them by a couple of tenths of a mile to make sure no one ducked in behind them. About half a mile behind Isaac, Danica and Hutch pulled surveillance as well. While Jackson stayed close to Everly and Amelia, Isaac and Danica would spend their time alternating between perimeter patrols and resting in a bunkhouse on the property. There would always be someone on duty.

The thought made Jackson feel a little better, but the pitch black of the wilderness among trees that blocked out the stars made him more than a little edgy. Even his headlights seemed dimmer, choked by the weight of the darkness.

For the past fifteen minutes, they'd ridden in silence. It was getting late, and he was exhausted. Everly was bound to be tired as well, and Amelia had dropped off to sleep in her car seat nearly an hour earlier.

The vehicle was quiet and peaceful, reminding him

of the road trips he'd taken with his family when he was a kid. His dad had been fond of late-night starts to "avoid traffic" so, while he took the wheel, the rest of the family had dozed until sunrise. Those had been the times in his life when Jackson had felt the safest.

It was too bad this time was nothing like those warmly remembered vacations.

He jumped when Everly touched his forearm. She'd moved to the front seat once darkness fell and it was clear Amelia was about to drop off.

It took all of his training not to slam on the brakes and reach for his sidearm. "Everything okay?" His voice was level, but it took a lot of effort to keep it that way.

"I'm fine, but can you stop for a second?" She pulled her hand back and pointed at something in the woods to their left, just outside of his headlight beams. "See those eyes?"

Jackson followed the line of her finger, relieved she wasn't carsick. Four eyes glinted in the dim glow of his headlights. "I do."

"It's a mama bear and a cub."

Jackson leaned forward, squinting. All he saw was reflected light, and then it was gone. "How do you know?"

"It's my job to know. I can tell a black bear and her cubs by how they move, how they stand, how they—" She dropped her hands into her lap and stared out the windshield. "Never mind. You can go ahead."

He almost urged her to keep talking, but then he lifted his foot from the brake and started forward. It was likely she'd stopped because she'd realized studying black bears was no longer her thing. It was no longer a topic she could even discuss with anyone. Any hint toward her life today could potentially tip someone off in her new life tomorrow.

As he rounded the last bend in the long trail to the site, the headlights illuminated a small but sturdy log cabin. It sat in the center of a clearing only slightly larger than the two buildings it housed. Letting the SUV coast to a stop close to the cabin door, Jackson killed the engine but left the headlights on. "We'll let Danica and Isaac scout the area before we head in. There's essentially no way anyone could have known we were headed out here, but just to be safe…"

"I'm used to it." She adjusted in the seat, settling in and stretching out her legs. "All these years and I still check under the beds and behind the shower curtains before I go to bed at night. Reasonably, I know the likelihood of someone being there is low, but it stops my brain from freaking me out at three in the morning."

"Makes sense." More than most people, Everly probably worried about a lot of thumps in the night.

The familiar headlights of Isaac's SUV appeared, with Danica's not far behind. His fellow officers squeezed into the clearing and exited their vehicles, retrieving their dogs from their kennels and heading off to search the property and the house. While Freddy could sniff out electronics such as bugs and bombs, Danica's partner, Hutch, was trained in suspect apprehension, a skill that could come in handy but Jackson hoped they wouldn't need.

Man, he missed Rex. Trained to protect, his partner would be the biggest asset of all. Tomorrow couldn't come quickly enough.

"Know what?" From the passenger seat, Everly turned to look at him. In the shadowy light from the headlights on the SUVs, her face was gray and tired. "I was just sitting here thinking I'd like a hot shower and to crawl into bed with the book I've been reading. It's a good one. I just hit a twist last night and couldn't wait to get into it tonight to find out what happens next. Guess I won't find out anytime soon." She pursed her lips and raised her eyebrows in what she probably thought was a comical expression. "I hope whoever stocked the cabin put a library in it."

"Not likely, although there might be a few paperbacks lying around. If you let me know the name of the book, I can reach out to whoever is bringing Rex tomorrow and see if they can bring you a copy."

Her expression relaxed. "You'd do that?"

It was a small thing that would bring her big comfort. If it was in his power to offer her some bit of normalcy, something to make her smile, he'd move mountains to do it.

This, however, was easy. "Get me a list of the books Amelia likes, too. We'll see if one or two of them can find their way into a bag of goodies. They're sending out supplies, so be sure to put down any foods you're partial to. What's in there now is canned goods." They also had a cooler of things like milk and eggs and cheese, which someone had scavenged from the break room and slipped into the SUV until real supplies could be brought in.

"Sweet." Sarcasm dripped from the word. "We'll make it work, though." Arriving at the cabin had relaxed her. Likely, the promise of a hot shower and sleep were working wonders on her emotional state. It was definitely working wonders on his. He was ready to drop, even if it wound up being on the floor.

As Danica rounded the house and headed for the bunkhouse beyond, her flashlight bobbing on the ground ahead of Hutch, the cabin's lights brightened the windows.

Isaac must be inside. They were one step closer to having Everly and Amelia secured behind closed and locked doors.

It was only a couple of minutes before Isaac opened the front door and waved them in, his beagle partner, Freddy, sitting at his heel with his tongue lolling out.

"Well, m'lady, are you ready to see your temporary castle?" Might as well try to lighten the mood.

Everly smiled, and it actually reached her eyes. "As long as it has running water and something remotely close to a bed, I'm more than ready."

Exiting the SUV and walking around to the passenger side, Jackson stood close as Everly opened the back door and gently extracted Amelia from her seat.

She eased out of the vehicle, cuddling the sleeping child close. "Can you grab the backpack on the back seat? It's the bag Tara packed for her of stuff she had at the house."

"Sure thing." As Everly stepped around him to walk the couple of feet to the house, Jackson reached in and picked up the backpack, which had been swept for tracking devices at headquarters. It would help Amelia to have a few familiar items during this turbulent time.

He walked into the cabin as a door closed on the far side of the room. The main living area was one large room with a small kitchen, a scuffed four-seat wooden table, and a sofa and side chair facing a small stone fireplace. The decor was straight out of the 1970s except for the refrigerator, which had been upgraded to white vinyl at some point. Two large braided rugs, predominantly red, sat in the center of what passed for the living room. Heavy red curtains hung over the two windows at the front of the house and over the two at the rear. There was no back door.

Although the Park Service kept up the cabins for emergencies, the slightly sweet and musty odor of a closed home made it feel like the place hadn't seen humans since the decade of disco.

He took in the rest of the space. The door Everly had closed behind her was likely the bedroom. A narrower door beside it had to be the bathroom.

And that was it.

Isaac was in the kitchen, taking inventory of the cabinets. "Good thing y'all ate on the way. Unless you're partial to canned soup or pork and beans, there aren't a lot of options."

"We've got the cooler in my vehicle. It's a start."

"Yeah, I saw Veronica put some cookies in the bag she packed out of the cabinets in the break room, too. I'm pretty sure everybody dropped something into your stash, and the cupboards are bare there now." Isaac grinned. "People lose their minds around cute kids."

Laughing, Jackson dropped onto the sofa and stretched his legs out under the rustic wooden coffee table. "I'm going to guess this is my bed for the night?" Fine by him. He always felt more in control when he was centrally located, not tucked off in a side room somewhere.

"You'd be guessing right. There's a closet in the bathroom with towels, blankets and sheets. They're in vacuum-sealed bags, so they ought to be clean, if a little stale."

The front door opened before Jackson could respond, and Danica entered with Hutch, whom she immediately directed to lie down by the kitchen table near Freddy. "Bunkhouse looks good. It's small and I had to chase out a few spiders, but we'll survive. There was a note that said the sheets and towels are here in the main cabin."

"Bathroom." Isaac walked into the living room and sat down on the chair, which sat at an angle to the couch. "You want first shift on patrol or second, Danica? I figure we'll each take six hours."

"Works for me. I can take the first shift. Hutch and I are wide-awake anyway." She moved toward the door, calling Hutch to her side. "We'll go ahead and move out. Both of you could stand to rest." Before they could say goodbye, she'd stepped out into the night.

Jackson felt instantly more relaxed. Someone else was on patrol. He could let his guard down slightly.

Because there was no telling what dangers the next day would bring.

Bright light dragged Everly out of a dead sleep. Her arms and legs felt as if they were weighted with concrete. Her brain was mush.

It took a few seconds to force her eyes open. As she blinked, letting her vision adjust to the light that was never this bright in her blackout-curtained bedroom, she began to take in her surroundings. Log walls. A dresser with a mirror mounted to the wall above it. A narrow door to the closet she'd peeked into last night. From somewhere nearby, voices spoke in low tones, though she couldn't make out words.

Beside her, Amelia slept on, her dark lashes fanning her cheeks.

Everly sighed and tried to move slowly so as not to wake her daughter.

Her surroundings were proof she hadn't merely had a nightmare. Kassandra Rennish really had found her, and she really was hiding deep in the Olympic Mountains.

With Jackson Dean.

Staring at a ceiling that bore multiple patches from previous leaks, she didn't stop her brain from walking along the path of Jackson's reappearance in her life. It was preferable to considering the danger she and Amelia were in.

One minute at a time.

For this one minute, halfway between dreams and reality, she wasn't going to control her thoughts.

Her eyes followed a crack in the ceiling. Jackson was as tall as she'd remembered, though he'd grown leaner and more muscular, likely due to the strenuous nature of his investigative job with the PNK9.

He still had incredible blue eyes that had always contrasted with his dark hair. His beard made the effect bolder.

She liked the beard. It made him look…ruggedly handsome.

Shaking off the thought, Everly gingerly sat up. *Nope.* Time to stop that line of thinking. Jackson was assigned to protect her…again. While they'd been unusually close given the nature of their relationship, he was still the man in charge of keeping her safe. Not a potential date. Definitely not someone she should be *noticing*.

She was too smart to fall for her rescuer like some fairy-tale damsel in distress.

Besides, this was temporary. The moment the Marshals felt it was safe, she'd be turned over to them and to her new life, never to see Jackson again.

The idea cut her. She'd mourned the loss of his presence in their lives once already. Doing it a second time, especially with Amelia growing attached to him now, was going to be harder than ever before.

The sound of an engine stopped her from thinking any further. It was the same kind of low hum the Park Service SUVs made.

Slipping from beneath the heavy quilt, she gently pulled it up over Amelia, who didn't even move. Maybe she'd sleep for a while longer and Everly could have a cup of coffee before she had to explain the reality of their situation to her daughter.

She looked down at the sleeping little girl, whose high cheekbones and long lashes were so much like her father's. Noah would have been so proud of her, and he'd have been gutted to know his decision to turn his boss over to the federal authorities had led to danger.

Everly smoothed the quilt, but her hand stopped halfway through the motion, her eyebrows drawing together. She'd been so exhausted the night before that she'd collapsed beside Amelia.

She definitely hadn't taken the time to find this quilt.

Someone had covered them during the night.

Jackson.

Her heart leaped at the thought. He'd always been protective of them, even outside of the realm of his job. His gentleness in the hospital had amazed her. He'd been a natural with Amelia, even though he'd confessed he'd never held a baby before, let alone changed a diaper.

That concern for others, the willingness to step outside of his comfort zone to go above and beyond the call of duty, made her feel warm inside. Jackson was a good man. They were blessed he was involved in their lives.

The scent of coffee drifted to her. A door opened, and a male voice spoke, louder than the others, before being shushed into silence. The sound of canine paws tapping on the wood floor indicated someone was up and about.

Normally, her day started before sunrise with time in her Bible and in prayer. While she had an all-weather Bible in her backpack, the thought of prayer made her skin hot with anger she was trying hard to keep contained. God had let her down. She had no words for Him at the moment.

Instead, she should join the group and find out what their next move was before she lost her nerve and curled up in a tight ball beneath the colorful quilt. Clearly, the last thing she needed was to be alone with her thoughts for too long. Fantasy, fear and frustration were nasty beasts that liked to leap upon her in the silence.

Smoothing her hair the best she could, Everly gave her sleeping daughter one last look, then slipped out the door into the living area of the cabin, which she'd been too exhausted to notice the night before.

The room was clean but dated, straight out of some sort of rustic *The Brady Bunch* episode. She half expected Jan to burst in with a "Marsha, Marsha, Marsha" lament at any second.

Instead, Jackson sat at a small table with a tired-looking Isaac and a younger man she hadn't seen before. All three nursed cups of coffee as though they needed the brew to survive. By the door, Freddy slept next to a German shepherd she didn't recognize.

Jackson looked up as she stepped into the room. "I was wondering if you were going to sleep all day."

"What time is it?" She acknowledged the other two men with a nod and headed for the kitchen and coffee. Until she'd downed at least part of a cup, socializing wasn't on her agenda. Truthfully, it wasn't on her agenda at all. She'd far rather spend the few quiet moments of this morning drinking coffee with Jackson alone.

She frowned as she poured coffee into a creamy white mug. Maybe having a full house was better after all.

As Everly settled the carafe back onto the warmer, she scanned the countertop. Several paper grocery bags covered the red Formica surface. A bag of marshmallows peeked out from the top of the one closest to her.

With a smile, she turned to face the table, leaning against the counter as she cradled the mug in her hands. "Are you really planning to make s'mores?"

All three men looked more than a little bit sheepish, but Jackson grinned through it. "Let's just say the team is a little soft when it comes to kids. There's more juice boxes and fruit snacks in those bags than real food."

"Amelia will be thrilled." She swung her gaze to the younger man she hadn't seen before. "Who's this?" Normally, she wouldn't be so abrupt, but it seemed as though a lot of people were aware of her whereabouts.

The man stood. He was tall and attractive, with not-too-short blond hair and striking green eyes. His smile was quick and friendly as he gestured toward the shepherd. "Owen Hannington, and that's Percy. I brought Rex to Jackson and was in charge of the grocery delivery. Also…" He dipped his chin. "I might be responsible for the chocolate chip cookies in the smaller bag."

Everly bit back a smile. She should be concerned about the amount of sugar her child was about to consume but, honestly, the gestures were all so sweet. "Thank you." She glanced around. "Rex is here?" If he was, she wanted to take a look at him and to see with her own eyes he was safe after charging into danger on her behalf.

As Owen resumed his seat, Jackson tilted his head toward the floor beside him. "He's over here. He's doing well, but he's still a little sleepy."

Setting her mug onto the counter, Everly approached. "Can I take a look at him?" When Jackson nodded, she knelt beside the Doberman, who opened one eye to look at her. His tail thumped twice before he closed his eye and relaxed.

"He remembers you." Jackson's voice came gently from above. "Owen said he slept all the way here. Kate says he'll likely sleep most of the day. He's supposed to take it easy until tomorrow, but I don't see there being much for him to do out here anyway."

Running her hands along the animal's back, she slid her fingers beneath Rex's front legs and took comfort in the strong, steady rhythm of his heart. It was so much stronger than it had been the day before. With two quick pats to his side, she rose and headed back to grab her coffee.

Behind her, chairs scraped against hardwood and Isaac spoke. "Freddy and I are going to head to the bunkhouse and get some sleep before our next shift. Owen, you should probably come along, too, if you're going to rotate in with us."

As she sipped her coffee, Everly's eyebrow went up along with her annoyance level. They were adding more people to this team? Why not just rent a billboard with her lat and long on it?

Jackson was obviously watching her. He gave her a slight shake of his head as he rose and followed the other two men to the door, closing it behind them. When they were gone, he grabbed his mug from the table and walked into the kitchen to refill it, then leaned against the counter beside her.

"Seems like there are a lot of cooks in this kitchen." Everly couldn't hide her frustration. She'd been down this road before. The fewer people who knew her location, the better.

"I understand, but we ran into an issue. Danica is needed back at HQ, so she'll be rolling out in a couple of hours, and someone had to bring Rex and supplies. Owen is familiar with the area and is just as trained as any of us in how to spot or evade a tail. No one followed him."

Everly tilted her head. "What do you mean by he's *just as trained as any of us*? Is he not part of your team?"

"Owen is part of a small group of candidates who are vying for two open spots in the PNK9 unit." Jackson held up his coffee mug between them to stop her from responding too quickly. "He's a highly trained law enforcement officer. He's no inexperienced rookie. If he was a slouch, he wouldn't have even been considered for a slot on our team."

The censure in his tone eased her ire. "I'm sorry. A lot is happening at once. I'm not handling curveballs well."

"I get it. So let's do this…" Switching his mug to his right hand, Jackson slipped his left arm around her shoulder and drew her close, similar to the way he'd done a time or two when she'd been overwhelmed in the past. "Take today and relax. You're surrounded by people who are more than capable of keeping you and Amelia safe. Let it be about helping her to feel safe and finding a way to break the news about all of the changes heading her way."

Somehow, being tucked into Jackson's side eased some of Everly's anger and fear, even though it shouldn't.

And he was right. Soon, she needed to find a way to tell her daughter they were never going home again.

EIGHT

Sparks from their small campfire caught the updraft and joined the smoke that lifted toward the sky. It almost looked as though the stars were being born in the fire and lofted skyward.

Jackson rolled his eyes. He was more tired than he thought if he was going poetic.

Yawning, he pulled his head to one side and then the other, stretching tense muscles in his neck. With all of its lumps, the ancient couch he'd slept on the night before wasn't exactly the epitome of comfort.

Not that he'd been inclined to sleep anyway. Every bump in the night had practically brought him to his feet. It hadn't helped he'd been aware of Rex's absence, either. He'd grown used to his partner's presence and counted on him to alert to danger.

Now Rex slept at his feet on the blanket. His back rested against Jackson's leg, which was stretched toward the fire. For a moment, with Isaac in the bunkhouse and Owen patrolling the perimeter, he could relax his vigilance slightly.

Closer to the small campfire, Everly hovered protectively next to Amelia, who was busy cramming her third s'more into her mouth.

The little girl reached sticky, chocolate-covered fingers to her mother's mouth to offer the last bite of graham-cracker-crusted goodness. "Have more, Mama."

Everly drew back with a huge fake frown and patted her stomach. "Mama is full from the first three. I think that's enough sugar for tonight."

"Okay." Amelia popped the bite into her mouth, then looked over her shoulder at Jackson. "Mr. Jack, want me to cook another marshmallow for you?"

Jackson grinned. He might not be a father, but he could see where this game was going. "I'm good, thank you." Amelia would roast marshmallows until dawn if her mother would let her, but the way Everly was guiding the conversation, she was thinking it was time for little girls to go to sleep.

Everly shot him a grateful smile over Amelia's dark hair and mouthed a *thank you*. Gently tugging on her daughter's braid, she slid back on the blanket to rest against the log, her shoulder nearly touching Jackson's. "Come on, firebug. Sit with Mama and Mr. Jack and see how big the stars are."

"Okay." Scooting over, Amelia let her mother clean her fingers with a damp paper towel. She stretched out beside Everly and planted her hands under her head, staring at the sky. "They're so bright."

The stars put on a show in the small circle above the clearing, filling the sky with twinkles of light. They were beautiful away from the cities' light pollution.

He should look up more often. Too often, he was scanning the ground for clues or keeping an eye on Rex, and he missed the beauty of his surroundings. It made him an excellent investigator, but it also made him miss out on so much.

Like the beauty in moments like this. Despite the chaos around them, there was peace with Rex on one side while Everly and Amelia lounged on the other. If he was the kind of person who allowed free rein to his imagination, he could almost pretend this was his life, with a wife and a daughter like the two he shared this moment with.

What would his life be like if he'd made different choices? Had taken the time to slow down and get to know a woman, to fall in love? Truth be told, Everly was the only woman who'd come close to his heart since, well… Since high school. He wouldn't deny she was the kind of woman he'd have chosen had he been free to choose.

Which he wasn't. He'd been driven as a deputy marshal and even more driven as a K-9 officer, urged forward by the vigilance necessary to protect those in his charge.

Particularly since he'd missed the signs and failed before.

"That was an awfully big sigh." Everly bumped his shoulder with hers. "What's on your mind?"

This woman pulled no punches. He liked that. And that quick brush of shoulder against shoulder? It had swirled something in his stomach he'd be better off ignoring. "Just catching my breath. And also?" He bumped her shoulder with his. He couldn't resist. "Men don't sigh. They exhale. Sighing is for romance novels and rom-coms."

"Right." The word held a hint of barely suppressed laughter. "If you say so."

He leaned forward. "Amelia, tell your mother men don't sigh."

"She's out." Everly rested her hand on the little girl's head. "She dropped off thirty seconds after she lay down."

It wasn't surprising. They'd spent the day exploring the small clearing around the house, then venturing a little beyond it to look for evidence of the black bears they'd seen the night before. While Jackson would have preferred to stay locked securely in the cabin, the short outings had been good for them.

This was likely Everly's last chance to study the animals she loved so much.

Amelia had impressed him with her knowledge of the outdoors, of woodland plants and the signs animals had been in an area. "You have a smart kid. She knows a lot for a four-year-old."

"We spend a lot of time on the trails. I hope that, wherever we wind up, hiking can still be a thing." Brushing hair from her daughter's forehead, Everly looked down at her. "She's at such a tough age for this. Old enough to realize things are going to be different but young enough to be honest in a very dangerous way." When she looked up, she caught Jackson watching her. "I don't know if this is going to work."

"Like I said, she's smart. You'll both be fine." They'd have to be. Jackson had let them go once before and he'd have to do it again very soon, but the idea of them not surviving this… It was more than he could take. "I was always invested in the two of you after everything that happened. I kept praying for you, even after we were no longer allowed to be in contact."

"You did sort of take on the father role in the hospital."

True. The nurses had actually called him *Dad* on

more than one occasion. Jackson hadn't corrected them. The situation had been too dangerous to raise questions.

Pulling her hand to her leg, Everly picked at a thread on the seam of her jeans. "I always thought we were… I don't know. Friends? And then one day you were gone. Short explanation. Brief goodbye." Her voice was tired and wistful.

Jackson couldn't look away. With her head tilted slightly forward and her focus intent on the thread, her hair had fallen forward to block her face. Not that it mattered. It was a face he'd never forget. One that sometimes haunted his dreams. Occasionally, those dreams involved moments like this, talking in the quiet, their relationship something more than it could ever be.

Those were the dreams he hated waking up from. Too often, he'd tried to go back to sleep so he could live there a little while longer, even though he shouldn't. He'd always chalked it up to the trials they'd been through together and the unusual circumstances of her transfer.

Now, the longer he was in her presence, the more he started to remember how she'd made her way into parts of his heart that should have stayed locked up tight.

He cleared his throat. The comment she'd made still hung between them, but he wasn't ready to discuss it. "I had to go. There were things happening outside of your case, and I couldn't remain in my position. It's a long story." One he'd never fully poured out to anyone. Sure, Ruby and a few others knew the basics, but he'd never delved into the pain or the fear that drove him on a daily basis because of Lance Carnalle's murder on his watch.

Right now, though, the story bubbled inside of him like a shaken soda can about to explode. He truly wanted to put his arm around Everly, draw her to his side and reveal the truth. To apologize for leaving her so abruptly. To tell her...

Well, to tell her he'd missed her. He'd never talked with anyone the way he'd wanted to talk with her. Had never shared the kinds of things he'd nearly shared with her as she'd recovered in her hospital room. Only protocol had kept him from opening up to her fully. Theirs had been a unique, strangely forged bond, and he hadn't realized a part of him was incomplete without her.

Instead, he crossed his arms over his stomach. "Speaking of what I missed, how about you fill me in on what the kiddo has been up to the past four years?"

When she tilted her head to look at him, her hair fell away from her face, revealing a small, sheepish smile. "True confession?"

"Sure. We've shared plenty of those in the past." He'd told her a few stories about his growing-up years, but nothing that had violated what he was allowed to say in his job. She'd told him about hers. She'd spoken of her grief over her husband's murder and having to leave her parents behind. He'd found himself bending the rules a bit and telling her about his grandfather's faith, which had influenced Jackson's own life.

Even though it was nearly dark in the dying firelight, there was a slight pinkness to her cheeks. "So, I have this shoebox at home and it's full of..." She sniffed and tipped her head toward the sky, giving him a glimpse of what she might have looked like at Amelia's age with her hand caught in the cookie jar.

"Full of...?" He poked a finger into her side, unable to resist teasing her when she looked so incredibly *adorable*. There was no other word for it. He wanted to let this warm feeling settle around him like a blanket.

With a chuckle, she edged away but immediately straightened. This time, because he'd turned toward her, her shoulder brushed his chest.

She didn't pull away.

Man, did he want to put both arms around her. The rush was like a crashing wave. He balled his fists against it and cleared his throat. "Full of…?"

When she took a deep breath, her shoulder moved against this chest. Yep, he definitely wanted to be closer. "It's full of letters about Amelia. Stories and milestones and…" When she turned her head to look him dead in the eyes, she was close.

Way too close.

So close he could hear her swallow before she spoke again, her voice a whisper. "They're addressed to you. I thought maybe someday, there would be a way to get them to you so you'd know…"

Her words. Her voice. Her touch. Each was a lightning bolt from his head to his toes. He felt his breath hitch.

Heard hers skip, too.

That lightning bolt had jumped between them. It lit a fire inside of him, illuminating things he'd never wanted to admit. Everly Lopez had worked her way into his heart.

And he might have worked his way into hers.

He searched her eyes, looking for answers to questions he didn't know how to ask…and finding them.

His hand slipped toward hers on the blanket and he let it trail up her arm to her shoulder to her cheek. And when she leaned forward, he let his lips brush hers, something he finally admitted he'd wanted for a long time.

Something that proved to himself he was a goner.

How long had she wanted to move a friendship with Jackson to something more?

It was a question without an answer. All Everly knew was, when his lips swept lightly across hers, something she hadn't felt in years gripped her heart.

But instead of kissing her fully, Jackson eased away with another loud exhale. He let his gaze sweep her face, then settled against the log and drew her close, resting her head on his chest, where his heart beat as fast as her own.

Everly closed her eyes and let herself rest in the safest place she'd known in years. She ought to feel disappointment he hadn't kissed her, but there was none. If he had, she wasn't sure what she'd have felt. But being held like this, in a way she hadn't been held since before Noah was murdered, she felt cherished and protected, as though someone had her back. Not only that, but that same someone wanted to be with her above anyone else in the world.

That someone was the man who had never really left her thoughts. When she'd been running for her life across the country, she was still grieving Noah's death. But as the months slipped by, her thoughts had often turned to Jackson Dean and the kind of man he had been to her and to Amelia. For months after he'd vanished, she'd ached more than she wanted to admit. She'd fooled herself into believing her feelings were a reaction to his selfless kindness. That she'd missed his friendship and the way they'd been able to talk to one another without reservation.

Now she knew…it had definitely been growing into something more.

Jackson said nothing. He didn't have to. He'd avoided kissing her for the very reasons that pounded in her own mind. They couldn't build anything together, not unless Jackson was willing to leave everything behind to disappear into WITSEC.

That was something she'd never ask him to do.

But in this moment, in front of the dying fire with the stars overhead and Jackson's heart beating against her cheek, she was going to pretend. After all, she was very good at pretending. The way she figured it, God owed her something good in her life before He let it collapse again. She was tired of building houses out of twigs. She wanted bricks. Or LEGOs. Those things were hard to take apart.

She ought to know. Amelia was fascinated with them.

"What's on your mind?" Jackson's voice was a low rumble against her ear.

Everly sniffed, half-amused at her answer. "LEGOs."

For a second, Jackson stopped breathing. "I'm really not sure how to take that." His voice was laced with humor, and he eased his arm from around her, letting her sit upright.

It was the last thing she wanted, especially as chilled Olympic air rushed in to fill the space between them, but it was the wisest thing they could do. If Amelia awoke and saw her mother resting in Mr. Jack's arms, it would set off all sorts of wild flights of fancy in the little girl who was lacking a father figure.

Everly crossed her arms against the cool night air, staring into the dying embers of the fire. "It was actually a compliment. I was thinking it would be nice to have something permanent, something not so easily kicked down during a toddler's tantrum."

The minute that last word dropped, Everly winced. In no way had she meant to hint at the feelings that had been bubbling inside of her for years. The way she'd worded the statement, it sounded like she wanted something permanent with Jackson.

Deep inside, in the secret and hidden places of her heart, she admitted life with Jackson would be something that surpassed special. But it was also something she could never have.

It was definitely something he hadn't even hinted at. All he had done was offer her a chaste kiss, then held her close, and she'd practically marched them down the aisle into forever.

Her cheeks heated. She'd sure stepped into that one. Sliding away from him, she crouched on her knees and leaned over Amelia. "I should get her inside. She really needs to sleep and, even though I keep putting it off, I'm going to have to tell her this isn't a vacation. It's a pit stop on the way to—"

"Everly." Jackson's hand rested in the center of her back, his palm warm through her lightweight sweatshirt.

She froze at the deep affection in his tone, but she didn't turn to him. He'd read her humiliation. He was good at things like that.

"Everly, I get it. Sometimes…" His fingers tightened, half gripping the fabric of her shirt before he dropped his hand. "Sometimes we want things we know we can't have."

The words dripped with a sadness that pricked tears behind her eyes. He couldn't possibly be talking about her... Could he?

"I'd like to explain why I walked away."

At the plaintive tone of the words, Everly eased back to sit, careful not to touch him. She'd wondered so often, and now she'd have answers, though she was no longer certain she wanted them.

Jackson watched the fire, clearly seeing memories instead of what was in front of him. He kneaded his knee as though it was causing him pain. More likely, it was the words he was about to speak more than any physical ache.

"It's short and bitter, really." The words were stronger than Everly had expected them to be. "I was assigned to several protected witnesses when I was on your case. It's likely you saw something about one of them in the news shortly before I saw you for the last time."

Something about one of them in the news...

Everly gasped. The story had been on all of the major networks. The star witness against a cartel leader had been killed by a car bomb, destroying the prosecution's case. For months, that event had made her tense every time she started her SUV. "Jackson..."

"I'm not looking for pity." He kept his gaze on the dying embers, probably seeing the aftermath of the bombing. "That man was my responsibility. He went somewhere he wasn't supposed to go, and it cost him his life. But do you know what? I knew it would happen. I knew he was thinking about going to the hospital. No matter what anyone says, it was on me. I was distracted, focused on something besides him, and it cost him his life."

Everly dug her teeth into her lower lip to keep a pained cry from escaping. Had she been the distraction? Had Amelia?

Not that it mattered. He'd left the job he had dedicated his life to because someone else chose to do the wrong thing. It wasn't his fault. "I've been there, in all of those trainings. They hammer into us the importance of following the rules, of not reaching out to the people we love. Our lives are in our own hands at that point. He knew going in what the risk was, and he took the risk. It's not your fault."

Pain drew tight lines around his mouth and eyes. "I still should have done something." With a quick head-shake, he stood. His next words rained down from above. "I'll carry Amelia in and then come back and bank the fire. You should probably sleep, too."

"Jackson, you—"

"No. Plenty of people have said what you're going to say. Let's just leave it alone." He stepped around her and knelt to lift her daughter, but he stopped when they were eye to eye, hesitating as he caught her gaze. The pain seemed to evaporate, replaced by something softer. "But those letters? About Amelia? If you don't mind, when the Marshals clear your place…" His gaze slipped to the side.

"I'll make sure you get them." There was no way she'd turn down the chance to pass them to the man they were intended for. She'd do anything to make him feel like he was worthy, to make him see the man he really was.

Besides, he clearly cared for her daughter. It had been obvious in the hospital, and it was obvious now, as he gently scooped her into his arms and cradled her close on the walk toward the cabin.

Everly trailed behind them. If life was different...

But it wasn't. And it never would be. Because Jackson carried too much pain, and she wasn't free.

Jackson didn't look at Everly as he rested Amelia on top of the quilt then left the room, closing the door behind him. As much as it felt like a dismissal, this was how it had to be.

Swallowing her anger at God and her sadness with the entire situation, she gently slipped Amelia into her pajamas. Her daughter was so exhausted, it was like stuffing cooked spaghetti into a drinking straw, drawing grins from both of their tired faces. When she finally got Amelia tucked in, she changed into the pajamas someone had sent along with Owen and slipped beneath the sheets.

But sleep didn't come. The anger building toward God seemed to gain heat with the cool of the night, burning her from the inside. *You could make it all go away. You could have kept us hidden. Could have saved Noah. Could have stopped all of this.*

She rolled onto her side away from Amelia, her breaths shallow and quick. Balling the quilt in her fist, she gripped it in a choke hold. *You could have kept me from feeling things for Jackson. Could have not dangled a future in front of me and jerked it away over and over again. You could have...*

The words were spent. Tears came instead, hot and furious, yet somehow also cold and sad. This was the kind of dual-edged pain she hadn't felt in a while. She'd forgotten how awful it was. If she could outrun it, she would, but there was no escaping it. Burying her face in the pillow, she tried not to let her shoulders shake. Amelia shouldn't be awakened by her mother's emotional outburst.

From the other side of the bedroom door, soft shuffles and the sound of paws on hardwood said Jackson had come back inside and was preparing to bed down on that horribly uncomfortable couch.

For her. He had given up the comfort of his own bed to protect her, even though he felt like a failed protector.

As the cabin fell silent, she rolled onto her back and stared at the ceiling, which was nearly invisible in the deep darkness of the forest. One more tear rolled down her temple into her hair. *God, I just want this to be over. I just want You to be here. To fix it.* She wasn't ready to apologize for her anger toward Him, but she needed to know there was something more in the room than the darkness and her own thoughts. *And please, help Jackson understand the truth about himself.*

The request for Jackson came easier than the ones for herself, but not by much. How did she talk to the God she'd trusted when He'd let her down? How did she lean on Him when she desperately wanted to but she was terrified of being disappointed? How did she handle it when the God she leaned on during hard times had—

Something scraped against the window.

Everly froze. Maybe it was Owen. Or a tree branch.

Except the house stood in the center of a clearing and no trees touched it.

Everly sat up, watching the window. Maybe she'd imagined—

A shadow shifted.

And Everly screamed as the window shattered.

NINE

Chaos.

Glass shattering. Everly screaming. Amelia crying.

Jackson leaped off the couch, where he'd been half-drowned in sleep, uncertain if he was awake or dreaming. Shaking off the fog, he unlocked the gun case on the coffee table and grabbed his weapon.

Rex raced over from his bed with more energy than he'd shown all day and heeled at Jackson's right hand, barking at Everly's bedroom door.

Another scream.

The door burst open and Everly launched herself from the room, Amelia in her arms. "Jackson!"

"I know. Go in the kitchen. Get behind the counter." Commanding Rex to follow, he ran for the bedroom. Where was his backup? Owen should be on patrol in a tight perimeter around the cabin. Why wasn't he here?

More glass shattered. Someone was coming through the window, and they didn't care who knew. They were either an amateur, or they were armed for battle and ready to sacrifice themselves for the prize.

He shook off the horrible reality of what *the prize* was. Everly. Dead.

Not on his watch.

Hopefully, the intruder wasn't counting on Jackson and Rex.

At the door, he stopped and motioned for Rex to heel. His partner waited beside him patiently, though Jackson could feel the tension of strained K-9 muscles ready to spring into action.

Rex was under strict orders to rest, so did he dare order his partner to attack?

Did he have a choice?

With a deep breath, he reached around the doorframe and flipped on the light, taking cover behind the wall.

The room fell silent.

Leading with his Sig, Jackson peeked around the doorway. A man wearing a mask and dark clothing had frozen with one leg in the room and the other outside. His eyes went wide and fixed on Rex.

"Federal agent!" Jackson leveled the pistol. "Stop and lace your hands behind your head!"

The man hesitated.

The last thing Jackson wanted was to fire. Of course, he had more than bullets on his side, and he had no other choice. "Rex. Attack."

With a bark that made even Jackson's neck hair stand on end, Rex launched himself across the room toward the man in the window.

Crying out a string of terrified curses, the man flung himself into the darkness. There was a thud as he hit the ground, then the scramble of dried leaves and branches as he ran across the clearing and into the trees.

"Rex. Halt." Jackson stopped his partner before he could follow out the window. With Rex still recovering, there was no way Jackson could safely put him onto the chase. "Guard." Pointing toward the living room where

Everly and Amelia were hiding, Jackson crawled out the window, trusting his partner to follow the command.

But once his feet hit the ground, frustration sapped his adrenaline. In the pitch black lit only dimly by the stars, he had no idea which direction to take to pursue the intruder. No way of knowing what was safe. The man could be hiding in the tree line waiting to take Jackson out with a single shot. Or he could be yards away in any direction. The woods had fallen silent.

Isaac was resting in the bunkhouse, but where were Owen and his German shepherd?

Climbing carefully back through the window, Jackson held his Sig behind his back as he reentered the living room, not wanting to frighten Amelia or Everly with the sight of it.

Near the kitchen, Rex stood facing the front door, his front legs spread slightly in preparation to move quickly if needed. From the other side of the bar between the kitchen and the living area, he heard soft singing and whispers occasionally punctuated by Amelia's sniffles.

Pulling his holster from the gun case, he slipped it on and stowed his Sig out of sight beneath the hem of his T-shirt. "Rex. Relax."

His partner immediately trotted to his bed and curled into a ball as though nothing had interrupted his rest.

After firing a quick text to Owen and Isaac, Jackson shoved his phone into his pocket and rounded the counter.

Everly and Amelia were huddled together in the corner by the sink. The little girl's face was pressed into her mother's shoulder, and Everly had turned her head to sing softly into her daughter's ear.

The fear on both of their faces ripped at Jackson's

heart. Not caring about the consequences, he settled on the floor and put one arm around each of them. "It's okay. He's gone." But for how long? Would he return with reinforcements to end Everly's life once and for all? It was tough to say, because the guy hadn't behaved like he was an experienced killer. People often panicked at the sight of Rex's sheathed ferocity though, so it was hard to know.

Not that it mattered. With the attacks coming swiftly and brazenly, either Kassandra Rennish had an army at her disposal, or the bounty on Everly's head was big enough to make dark web assassins take notice.

It seemed the guy tonight had been acting alone. Otherwise, the attack would have been more coordinated. A bounty was the likely motivator, which made the situation even more dangerous. Fighting a coordinated group was one thing. Going to war against a series of lone attackers who cared about nothing but themselves and their wallets was an entirely different matter.

Everly leaned against him, her shoulders losing some of their tension as he held her. Even Amelia seemed to sense Jackson would go to any lengths to keep them safe. Her sniffles faded as she relaxed in her mother's arms.

After a moment, Everly pulled away and looked up at him. Her expression was a mixture of fear, anger and determination, the lines around her mouth and across her forehead writing the story of her pain.

She knew what came next. They were moving again.

Before Jackson could speak, someone pounded on the cabin's only door. "It's Isaac and Freddy."

With a quick squeeze of Everly's shoulder, Jackson rose and strode to the door, unlocking it to let the pair in. There was still no response from Owen. Either he was slacking in his duties or...

Jackson didn't want to consider what the intruder might have done to Owen before attempting to enter the cabin.

Isaac glanced around the room, his expression hard yet tinged with concern. "Where's Owen?"

"Right here." Owen and his German shepherd, Percy, stepped into the cabin behind Isaac. "I didn't find the suspicious vehicle you were talking about."

Jackson's relief at Owen's safety evaporated. "What suspicious vehicle?"

Whirling on Owen, Isaac reached around him and shut the door. "Where were you?" He lowered his voice when Jackson tapped his arm and tilted his head toward the kitchen, where Everly and Amelia remained on the floor out of sight. "You were supposed to be close to the house. Perimeter detail."

Owen retreated so quickly his back hit the door. He held up his hand as Percy heeled at his side. "Whoa. I was right where Jackson told me to be." Reaching into his pocket, he pulled his phone out and pressed the screen, then held it up toward Isaac and Jackson.

Jackson's name appeared at the top of a text thread. The second-to-last text was one he didn't recognize. NPS reports suspicious vehicle east of cabin about a thousand yards. Investigate. I'll watch here.

Jerking his phone from his back pocket, Jackson punched the screen. There was the message, just as it appeared on Owen's phone.

How? His phone had been on him the entire time. He passed it to Isaac. "I didn't type that." He pinched the bridge of his nose. Sure, he'd been half-asleep, but he certainly hadn't been gone enough to forget he'd sent a text.

Isaac shook his head. "Cell phones and texts are nothing but trouble."

"What?" The comment seemed totally out of place, given the circumstances—and the fact that Isaac and his partner specialized in electronics.

"It's too easy for good hackers to break into even seemingly secure phones." He shook his head. "And I got dumped by text once, a long time ago. It wasn't pretty." He shoved the phone back toward Jackson. "Look, I know you want to keep the circle tight, but it might be time to have all hands on deck." Isaac dropped his hand heavily onto Jackson's shoulder. "The whole team needs to know what's going on, and then we need to get you guys somewhere safe. The more eyes we have, the better."

Nodding, Jackson let Isaac take the lead on setting up the meeting as Owen dropped into a chair and stared at the wall. There wasn't time to deal with him at the moment. "Go out to the bunkhouse and see if you can find something to board up the window before a bear or something gets in."

With a nod, Owen left, his shoulders slumped. It was tough to blame the guy. A string of unfortunate incidents had happened with the four new candidates, ranging from the annoying to the dangerous. Some on the team thought it was just coincidence. Others felt like there was a saboteur among them. Someone had gotten Owen out of the way when Jackson needed him. Rennish or her goons? Or had one of the other candidates been behind it, to make Owen look bad?

He didn't have time to dwell on that. Instead, he

walked into the kitchen and found Everly with her head bent over a sleeping Amelia. She lifted her eyes when he drew near. "I wish I felt safe enough to drop off again." The words were meant to be light, but they had a hard edge, one that revealed her fear and anger.

Jackson settled beside her, his shoulder resting against hers. "Want to move to the couch? I can take Amelia."

"No." She leaned heavily against him. "I'm afraid she'll wake up and, with no bedroom to move her to…" Everly dipped her chin toward her chest. "I don't want to do this anymore."

"I know." It was all Jackson could do not to put his arm around her again. His muscles physically ached to do so, to offer her the silent promise of protection and safety.

But he didn't. There were too many lines he wanted to cross, and they took his focus off his primary job of protecting her. He couldn't let her presence or his emotions distract him from the task at hand. Not if he wanted Everly and Amelia to survive.

"Explain to me how this happened." Normally easygoing but firm, Chief Donovan Fanelli was all hard lines and chiseled edges, his blue gaze icy as he eyed each member of the PNK9 on the screen. Behind him, a sterile hotel room nearly identical to the ones behind both Ruby and Peyton revealed they were still out of town in search of the missing pups. Isaac had reached out to Donovan, who had gathered most of the team online within fifteen minutes. Jackson had just finished briefing the team on Everly's situation.

All of them were alert and listening, even though each appeared to have been awakened from sleep. Since it was well past midnight and their days started early, that wasn't surprising.

Given how exhausted Jackson was, it was likely both Isaac and Owen, who stood behind him watching the screen of Isaac's computer on the kitchen table, looked as bad as everyone else felt.

"What happened?" The chief repeated his question, punching the words harder this time.

Owen leaned closer to Jackson, peering over his shoulder at the screen but not looking directly into the camera. "The only thing we can figure is this is my fault."

Across the screen, expressions hardened. This was the latest in a series of headaches involving the candidates competing for slots within the K-9 unit. While they'd started out close, fractures had developed among them. Just a few weeks earlier, Veronica Eastwood's badge and gun had been moved, costing her an opportunity to question a suspect with another officer. There had been rumblings that, because she was their tech expert's younger sister, she was already a shoo-in for the job.

Veronica stared directly at the camera as though her deep brown eyes could see straight through it into all of their thoughts, but she said nothing. It wasn't hard to guess what she was thinking, though. Here was another misstep by a candidate. Was it by accident, or was someone out to sabotage them?

Jackson dragged his hand down his face as the chief spoke again. "What mistake did you make, Owen?" It was tough to tell if he was seeking information or using this near-deadly incident as a teaching point.

Owen shook his head. "I really thought no one followed me out here. I took all of the necessary precautions. This isn't my first time working to evade a tail, but—"

"I'm more concerned about the reason you weren't in position near the cabin tonight." Again, the chief's voice held a knife's edge.

Jackson cut in. "That's the weird part." He searched the screen for Jasmin's face and addressed her image. He hated video calls, but it made him feel more connected to his teammates if he looked directly at who he was speaking to instead of at the camera. "Jas, maybe you can help us."

"Fire away."

He held out his hand to Owen, who unlocked his phone and deposited it onto Jackson's palm. Jackson held the phone up to the camera. "Owen received a text from me instructing him to step away from the cabin." When Jasmin leaned closer to the screen and then nodded, Jackson held up his phone. "It's right here on my phone, but I never sent that text. And before you ask, my phone hasn't been out of my sight or reach since Ruby handed it to me."

"I took a cursory look at the phone and didn't spot anything obvious," Isaac added.

Eyes narrowed, Jasmin scanned the screen then sat back in her chair, clearly deep in thought. She propped her elbow on the chair and rested her head on her hand, covering her mouth. Her index finger tapped her upper lip. It was a moment before she spoke. "Without the phones in front of me, I can't say what's going on, but I can dig into phone records and try to see if something weird pops up. It's tough to say how someone spoofed it and managed to make it land in a text string you guys had already established, though."

That was his thought as well, though he wasn't as technically minded as Jasmin and Isaac were.

The chief straightened. "Owen, no doubt you messed up tonight. You didn't verify the message, either by responding to it or by stepping into the cabin to check with Jackson directly. That was a rookie mistake, one I wouldn't expect from someone with your law enforcement background."

Owen stiffened, but he didn't speak.

On-screen, Veronica muttered something the mic picked up, but the words weren't loud enough to make out.

"You have something to add, Veronica?" The chief's eyes shifted as he watched the screen.

"It's just…" Her expression morphed from sheepish to defiant. "It's just… Owen and I have both had weird things happen, almost like someone wants us to fail. And Parker? Nothing's happened to him."

"Whoa." Parker Walsh held his hands up in front of him. His dark hair was mussed as though he might have been awakened from sleep. "That was uncalled for."

But was it? Jackson stared at the younger man. Parker was a solid law enforcement officer, competent and intelligent, but he was also prone to bragging about his past accomplishments. Was he just naturally proud, or was he covering up for something?

"Think about it." Parker lowered his hands and stared directly into the camera. "Brandie's not had anything bad happen to her, either, so—"

"Seriously?" Normally quiet, Brandie Weller's voice fired through the speakers. She was a bright candidate, though her interest in child abduction cold cases seemed to distract her. Word had spread that in her off time, she was often seen researching old reports and files. "I'm not—"

"I'm sure it's coming." Veronica cut in. "It seems like Parker was the one who gained from my missing gun and badge. And now it's—"

"Hold up." Jackson's voice came out more savage than he'd intended, but he had no patience or time for bickering that was, frankly, childish and beneath trained law enforcement officers. "We can't change what's happened. The fact is, we've been compromised. I need to move Everly and Amelia as quickly and safely as possible. And by quickly, I mean immediately. Within the half hour." Whatever, if anything, was happening within the candidate group, it wasn't of immediate concern.

Everly and Amelia had been sitting ducks long enough already. Whoever had broken into the house had confirmation they were in the cabin and likely knew a relocation would happen tonight. The window for another attack was closing, and the guy was still out there. The question wasn't whether or not he'd return. The question was whether or not he'd return with superior firepower. With a big enough bounty in place, an assassin wouldn't hesitate to take down law enforcement officers who stood in his way. None of them were safe.

"He's right." The chief's tone left no room for further discussion. Brandie, Parker and Veronica all avoided looking straight into the camera. Although Owen had remained out of the fray, Jackson could only imagine he was doing the same since he'd stepped out of view of the camera.

"What do we do?" Isaac leaned in closer to Jackson so the others could see him.

The chief reiterated the situation, just enough to let

the team know this was volatile and dangerous. Then he drummed his fingers on the table. "Jackson, I'll arrange another safe house. Isaac, you stick close to Owen. You two will escort Jackson to the next location when I have it, then you'll head back here. Isaac, I'll have you return to meet Jackson after he's relocated."

What the chief wasn't saying was Isaac was escorting Owen and a chat was likely forthcoming. He wouldn't want to be in Owen's shoes right now.

The chief continued talking. "Jackson, I'll call Isaac with instructions on where you're headed next, then he'll lead the way so we keep your phone out of play."

"You think it's been compromised? Neither Isaac nor I could find any evidence it had been." Still, he'd ditch the thing right now if it had. "Jasmin just formatted it brand-new yesterday."

"No, but let's not take any chances." The chief's gaze roamed his screen. "If any of you receive a text message related to this case or any other, you call to verify. Every theory is in play about who or what drew Owen away from the house. It could have been someone after Jackson's witness. It could have been someone disrupting the candidate selection process. It could also be someone with a vendetta against the PNK9. We have enemies, you know." He picked up a pen and jotted something out of sight. "Jack, I'll send an investigative team out to search for evidence once you're on the move. We'll figure this out and stop it, somehow, some way."

"I know how." From the kitchen, Everly's voice drifted over. She stood at the end of the bar, a sleeping Amelia in her arms. Her face was a mask of determination, but Jackson could read the words she was about to say.

He stood. "Everly, no. Listen. You're not—"

"No. *You* listen." She stepped closer, stopping about six feet away. "I want this to end." She stepped around him and stood between him and camera. "Chief Fanelli, I want my life back, and my daughter safe. Use me as bait."

TEN

"Absolutely not." Jackson slammed the laptop shut on the active video call.

Isaac jumped, probably because it was his computer. "Jackson, why—"

"He didn't want anyone to hear what I said." Everly turned, walked away and gently laid Amelia on the couch.

As Jackson's phone started to ring, she came back and stood watching him, challenging him to argue with her.

He didn't move. It didn't even appear he was breathing. Only the storm behind his blue eyes betrayed his emotions.

But it didn't look like anger.

No, it looked like fear.

Everly should know. It was an emotion she lived with day and night, a constant presence that controlled every move she made.

Well, not any more.

The phone went silent.

"Guys." Owen stepped in, forming an awkward triangle. "I am so sorry. I really thought no one followed me. When it comes to the text, I should have checked. This is my fault. I don't know how—"

"Walk away." Jackson ground out the words from

deep in his throat, hardly moving his mouth. His jaw worked as though he was chewing on his next words.

Owen had better heed Jackson's command.

"Let's go." Grabbing his laptop, Isaac tugged Owen's sleeve. "We'll keep the perimeter secure and then roll out when the chief calls." He set his computer on the bar out of Jackson's reach, then called to Freddy.

With a last apologetic look at Everly, Owen called Percy and followed Isaac, shutting the door softly behind him.

"No." Jackson's refusal echoed the click of the latch. It brooked no argument.

Well, he didn't know her at all if he thought one word was going to stop her. Everly drew back her shoulders so she stood at her full height. Although she only came up to Jackson's chin, she prepared for battle. "This ends now. If I show myself, they'll come after me and you can take them into custody. They don't want me dead. The guy at the bridge said—"

"There's your problem. You think we can take one person into custody and be done." Dragging his hand across the top of his head, Jackson paced to the door. "We might catch a break and apprehend one person. *One.* You can't even assume everyone gunning for you is working for Rennish. Jasmin is searching the dark web to see if there's a bounty on your head. There could be a dozen freelancers looking for a quick buck."

Everly's heart skipped. A faceless, numberless mob seemed to gather around the cabin, waiting to attack.

So he might be right, but still... There had to be something she could do.

When he turned, his expression had softened into

sympathy. "I get it. You want to be safe." He jerked his chin toward the sofa. "You want Amelia to be safe."

Everly refused to break eye contact.

"Unless we can find a way to take down Rennish, you'll still be in danger."

"Then draw her out. Tell her I'll surrender if she'll leave my child alone and—"

"She didn't get to the heights she reached by being stupid. She knows you're with us. There's no way she'll show herself, not even for revenge. She's not that hands-on."

Jackson was wrong. "She was with Noah." Emotion choked the words. "Because Noah was gathering evidence and had to stay under the radar, he wasn't under witness protection. She knew what Noah was doing. She walked right in my front door, and…" Everly pressed her palms to her eyes, wishing she could erase the horror she'd witnessed from the top of her stairs. That she could overwrite the sound of the gunshot that had left her husband bleeding out on the hardwood floor.

There was no need to finish the story. Jackson already knew it.

There was a footstep, then she was in Jackson's arms, her hands trapped between her face and his chest.

No, not *trapped*. Sheltered. In the circle of his embrace, it was easy to believe she was safe.

No tears fell. She'd wept herself dry. Had forced herself to move forward.

She'd do it again, too.

On the table, Jackson's cell phone rang, but he didn't move. Instead, his shoulders rose and fell with a deep breath. He tipped his chin, and his words brushed the top of her head. "Have you prayed about this?"

Her muscles stiffened. No, she had not, and she wasn't going to. Rotating her hands, she pressed her palms to Jackson's chest and shoved gently, causing him to drop his arms. "Why should I?"

"Everly…"

"No, really. Why should I? I've been praying for years. Look where it got me. It's no business of His if I want to stop this. He's not doing anything."

"You know that's not how it works. Bad things happen." Jackson stepped closer. "We'll probably never know why this is happening. But you can't just turn your back on Him."

"Watch me." Defiance coursing hot through her, she turned away from Jackson. Hopefully, he'd see the symbolism. "At the moment, I don't care what He has to say."

"Understandable." From the sound of his voice, Jackson hadn't moved. "I felt that way when my witness died."

Turning slowly, Everly eyed him. "What did you do?"

Jackson scanned the ceiling, his arms crossed over his chest. "Nothing, at first. But then I reached the place where the anger was so big I couldn't hold it in, so I was honest with Him. I told Him I was furious and I didn't want to talk to Him. I didn't trust Him."

So Jackson had railed at God, yet here he stood, unscathed. She cleared her throat. "Then what happened?"

"It was like I'd broken through a wall and I could talk to Him again. At first, it was a lot of spouting off reasons He was wrong. Gradually, like any relationship, we moved forward. It took a long time, and what you're going through is harder."

That was all well and good, but she wasn't there yet. Everything was too raw, and she had no desire to pray.

"I'll think about it." Whether *it* was talking to God or putting herself out there to draw Kassandra Rennish from hiding, she wasn't sure.

A soft ring broke the stillness. His phone again.

Everly turned to check on Amelia. "You should answer it, and I should pack."

"This conversation isn't over."

"I didn't think it was." With a quick scan of her sleeping daughter, Everly headed for the bedroom to shove their few possessions into their backpacks.

"When?" The harsh tone of Jackson's voice shattered the silence. When she turned, he was staring straight at her, his jaw set and his expression a storm of pain.

He hadn't been entirely truthful with Everly.

Jackson navigated a curve in the road as the first signs of a new day softened the darkness. Deep in the Olympic National Park they wouldn't see the sunrise, but a change in the air subtly indicated dawn was approaching.

He checked the rearview. No one was behind them unless they were following without headlights, a dangerous game along these roads.

In the cargo area, Rex snored softly. Likewise, Amelia slumbered in her car seat.

Only Jackson and Everly were awake. She sat in the back seat with her head against Amelia's car seat and her eyes closed, but the pace of her breathing said she was awake.

She was ignoring him because she knew he was hiding something.

Letting one hand fall to his leg, Jackson massaged his knee, which had started bothering him earlier in the day, probably from his leap into the river. It wasn't painful, but it twinged just enough to remind him it existed.

Kind of like his conscience. But there was no way he was going to tell Everly what the chief had said when they'd talked after the video call ended.

Someone had set fire to her small house, and the extent of the damage was currently unknown. Fortunately, a team with WITSEC had already retrieved a few things, but the rest…?

The viciousness of the attack clawed at his heart. Such an act went beyond cruelty. It was a warning. Kassandra Rennish wanted to destroy not just Everly herself but everything about her identity.

It was also a deadly threat. If Rennish couldn't get her hands on Everly directly, she'd destroy everything related to her. This was an escalation.

PNK9 had coordinated with the Marshals Service to move Everly's friend Tara and her family to a safe house, taking every precaution against a blow to Everly's nearest and dearest. Local law enforcement had set up additional patrols around her church, and the Park Service was keeping a close eye on the office where Everly had worked. Rennish was getting desperate to draw Everly out, and collateral damage wouldn't be a deterrent.

Jackson had initially believed Rennish wouldn't come after Everly directly, but now he wasn't sure. Her desperate actions were the work of a woman unhinged.

He'd chosen to tell Everly only that someone had made a threat against her home. In Everly's current state, the news of the fire would likely be more than she could take.

So if telling half the truth protected her emotions,

he'd do it gladly and deal with the fallout later, when she learned the whole story.

For now, they were on the road again. They'd rendez-voused with a team that had been dispatched to one of the Stark Lodges at the entrance to Olympic National Park. Acting as a decoy, Officer Colt Maxwell and Of-ficer Candidate Veronica Eastwood had set out with two escort vehicles, headed to a Park Service cabin about an hour in the opposite direction from the route Jackson was driving.

Hopefully, they'd drawn any possible tails.

He'd set off with Everly and Amelia ninety minutes after they left, with Officer Dylan Jeong and his part-ner, a Saint Bernard named Ridge, about ten minutes behind him. With only Jackson visible in the front seat and Everly and Amelia hidden behind tinted glass, no one should realize he was chauffeuring the real targets.

This time, they wouldn't be staying in a Park Service cabin. Anyone who had access to the system could find those and, if Rennish was smart, she'd have her people systematically searching them.

The chief had a fishing buddy who had a cabin above Lake Crescent. Although the property was in the park, it was a privately owned inholding, created when Congress drew the park boundaries without pur-chasing all of the land within. Because it wasn't a Park Service cabin, it provided a hidden place to land until WITSEC believed it was safe to retrieve Everly and Amelia.

His phone vibrated in his thigh pocket, and he tapped the Bluetooth headphones in his ear. He hadn't con-nected his phone to this temporary SUV, and he didn't want Everly to hear his conversations anyway. "Jackson Dean."

"Hey. It's Jasmin."

Something in their technical expert's tone made him straighten. When he glanced into the rearview, Everly hadn't moved.

Maybe she was asleep after all.

"What's up?" He kept his voice neutral. If Everly was awake, he didn't want to tip her off to his conversation. She didn't need any more stress.

"Let's just say things aren't what we initially thought."

"Okay?" He really wasn't in the mood for cryptic.

"I've scoured the dark web. Combed through records from the FBI and the task force that took Rennish down. One thing has become blindingly clear."

"Wait." They were in the midst of several high-profile cases as well as searching for their missing bloodhounds. Jasmin was already stretched to the limit, but clearly she'd turned resources and energy toward an assignment that wasn't technically hers. "Have you slept at all?"

"Haven't you heard?" She chuckled, the sound jarring given their situation. "Sleep is for the weak."

"Wrong." She needed to rest soon or she'd be no good to any of them. At the moment, though, he needed to hear what she had to say. "What's become clear?"

"Kassandra Rennish is broke."

Jackson let the words settle, then began to run the implications through every investigative filter he had. No money meant no dark web bounty that sent an untold number of assailants on a treasure hunt with Everly as the prize. Rennish likely had little help outside of a handful of dedicated hangers-on who believed she could eventually offer them something more. Or she'd convinced a few thugs she could pay when the score was settled.

In one way, this was good news. It narrowed the field of possible assailants and made it easier to hide.

But in another way, this was the worst possible news. Kassandra Rennish had been a very rich woman before Noah had taken his discovery of her trafficking operation to federal authorities. Everly's eyewitness testimony concerning her husband's murder had put the kingpin away. "Any clue how it all went away?" He worded the statement as carefully as possible to avoid tipping Everly off that he was talking about Rennish.

"Her second-in-command saw his opportunity and walked away with everything. Dale Hurston wiped out her accounts, dismantled her organization and vanished. He likely dropped off the radar to avoid Kassandra more than to avoid prosecution."

So Hurston had double-crossed Rennish, but he was in hiding. That meant Rennish was unleashing her anger on Everly.

This was definitely personal.

Everly might be right. Given that Rennish had personally murdered Noah in his own home, she might come after Everly to deal with this herself.

Again, it was a double-edged sword. They were dealing with a woman who had nothing to lose, but they were also dealing with a killer who might show herself in a way that allowed them to stop her before she could kill again.

"I heard Everly volunteered to—"

"No." As ruthless as Kassandra Rennish was, there was no way to ensure Everly's safety if she was used as bait. It also went against everything he'd learned as a deputy marshal and as a law enforcement officer.

He'd seen what happened when a witness stepped out into the open. There was no way he was going to risk Everly's life with such a scheme. He'd never survive if he not only lost her, but if he also had her blood on his hands.

ELEVEN

Well, this cabin was definitely preferable to the last one.

Everly stood at a large window that looked out over Lake Crescent. While there was a lodge on the lake, and it was often frequented by tourists, the cabin sat in the side of the mountain above a quieter section. The still lake surface reflected the sky above, making it seem as though the clouds had fallen to earth.

The three-bedroom cabin was ringed by trees, creating an oasis of calm in the storm her life had become.

With Jackson and an officer named Dylan outside scouting the area with their partners and Amelia coloring at the table, the house was quiet. She'd be sure to have Jackson thank whoever had sent the toys and books that gave her daughter a sense of normalcy.

The floor creaked, and a voice followed quickly. "You know you can't stand there forever. You're wide open to view from any number of directions." From behind her, Jackson's voice shattered the peace and dragged her into the horror that was her new reality.

Well, her old reality made new again.

He was right, though. At the moment, she was probably safe to soak in the view as long as she wanted, because the bright sunlight outside prevented a casual observer from seeing too deeply into the cabin. But if anyone had binoculars or a rifle scope trained on the place…

With a bone-deep shudder, she walked away from the window, dropping onto a sofa ten times more comfortable than the one at the Park Service cabin had been. "This is an upgrade. I'm pretty sure the Park Service doesn't own this property. Is it an inholding?" Nearly every park in the country was dotted with private land that held everything from houses to gas stations. It was a source of contention for some and a source of pride for others.

Everly had never formed a solid opinion about "inholders" one way or the other, but she had always envied pristine views that came with living in a home encircled by protected land.

"It's private. The place belongs to a friend of the chief's. It started out back in the 1800s as a hunting cabin. When the Park was formed in 1938, the guy's great-great-whatever-grandfather opted to let the park build around him. They've added on and renovated and upgraded over the years, always keeping it within the trees so it doesn't detract from the view of others around the lake. They've even remained largely off the grid with solar panels and rain barrels and such. It's a fishing cabin, basically."

"Compared to the last place, it's the lap of luxury. You even get to sleep on something comfortable." Although she was annoyed with him for shooting down her offer to save herself and Amelia, she was glad he would be able to upgrade to a bed instead of that awful sofa.

She was also grateful they wouldn't have to share a bathroom. The bedroom she was sharing with Amelia had its own bathroom, while the two rooms Dylan and Jackson were using on the other side of the small living area shared one.

They'd brought along their provisions, but this cabin was also stocked with canned and dry goods as well as a deep freeze filled with fish and meat. According to Dylan, they'd been granted permission to eat freely from all of it.

She might even cook tonight. Anything would be preferable to the hot dogs that had sat like a rock in her stomach the night before.

"Mama?" From the kitchen table, Amelia's voice rose plaintively.

Everly's forehead creased. Her daughter was using her soft *I'm sad* voice.

Everly's eyes skipped from Amelia to Jackson and back again before she rose and went to sit in the chair next to Amelia's at the small table. "What's up, buttercup?" The endearment never failed to make Amelia smile.

Today, though, the smile was more like a flash of lightning, there and gone before Everly could fully acknowledge she'd actually seen it. "Mama, when are we going home?"

Everly's breath caught. She'd been dreading this moment for what felt like years, and there was no way to put it off any longer. Her daughter deserved the truth, although it would have to be couched in terms a four-year-old could understand.

How did she do that? *God, help me. Help Amelia. We need You to get us through this.* The words were unbidden and automatic. She clamped down on her lower lip, almost as if doing so could keep her from continuing a conversation with God. She wasn't talking to Him, and yet she still needed Him. *This doesn't mean I've stopped being mad at You*, she grumbled inwardly, then almost smiled. He knew. She didn't need to tell Him.

"Well, baby, here's the thing. We—"

"Can I talk to you for a second?" Jackson's voice cut through the words she was making up as she went along.

She ought to be angry he'd stepped in to this difficult moment, but she had no clue what to say to her child. If he had something to offer, then she'd gladly step aside and let him speak. After all, he'd been with them at the beginning of this years earlier. He was the man who'd helped to guide Amelia through her first days in the world. Maybe him being involved now was natural.

Everly laid her hand on Amelia's wrist. "Can you color for a second while I talk to Mr. Jack?"

With a solemn nod, Amelia lifted a turquoise crayon and poised it over the page. "Okay. But then I want some answers."

It sounded like Jackson choked on air.

An unexpected laugh forced Everly to press her lips tightly together, the mirth a deep rumble trapped in her throat. Where had her daughter even heard that phrase?

When Everly thought she could speak without looking as though she was laughing at her child's soberness, she nodded. "Answers on the way, ma'am."

She avoided Jackson's gaze as she rose and walked into the large open kitchen on the far side of the room. If he had even one spark of amusement in his eye, she'd lose it.

He followed close behind, and she walked to the sink,

bracing her hands on either side of it as she stared out the window. "I can't look at you."

"I understand." There was amusement in his voice, but then he took a deep breath and it seemed as though the air around them changed. "But we need to talk about something before you say anything to Amelia."

Something else had gone wrong. It thickened the tension more with every passing second. Pressing her fingers into the lip of the counter, she braced herself. "What happened?"

"The short version, since Amelia is waiting…" He drew in an audible breath. "The Marshals moved personal items out of your home within hours of me finding you, but after they were gone…" His warm hand rested heavily on her shoulder, turning her toward him.

She didn't want to look at him or to acknowledge what might come next. This was all too hard, but she forced herself to raise her eyes to his.

It was the first time she'd genuinely looked him in the eye since the night before. Had he slept at all? Dark circles ringed his eyes. There was pity and concern in his gaze.

She wanted to sink into the peace of having someone care about her, but she didn't dare. When she let her guard down, bad things happened. "What is it?"

His grip tightened as though he was going to draw her to him, but then he let his hand fall to his side. "Someone set fire to the house. I don't know the extent of the damage, but…"

Sagging against the counter, Everly waited for the body blow more bad news should bring. Waited for the pain of knowing her home was gone.

There was nothing. Numb emptiness gutted her,

leaving behind an empty skeleton. No pain. No fear. No sense of loss. Just hollow, echoing nothingness.

The absurdity almost made her laugh. She'd already lost the house. The Marshals had already retrieved her belongings. Burning the place was a sheer act of cruelty that changed nothing.

She was never going back there anyway. It was simply…extra. Too much. The thing that pushed her out of her emotions and into a free-floating rationality that almost seemed to disconnect her from reality.

"Everly?" Jackson dipped his chin. "What's going on in there?"

With a humorless smile, she shook her head. "In a way, Kassandra Rennish just made everything easier." On her, maybe, but certainly not on her daughter.

"How?" Jackson's question chased her as she stepped around him and walked back to the table to sit beside her daughter.

Amelia slid the crayon back into the box and looked at her mother with a tilt of her head. "Is this a vacation? And when are we going home?" There was longing in the words. "I want my bed and Mr. Ursa."

Oh, how she hoped a marshal had been child-aware enough to grab Amelia's favorite large stuffed black bear from his resting place against her pillows.

Reaching for her daughter, Everly pulled Amelia into her lap and snuggled her close against her chest. She was almost too big for such cuddles, but Everly would draw them out for as long as she could. Right now, she needed to hold her daughter as much as her daughter needed to be held. "Baby, do you remember a few months ago, when your friend Riley's house burned down?"

In January, a family from church had lost everything in a fire, and the congregation had rallied around them to provide support and necessities as they grieved and ultimately decided to relocate closer to family in Seattle.

Amelia nodded slowly. "We gave some of my clothes to his sister. And some of my toys I didn't play with anymore."

"Exactly. They found a new house in a new city, and they went to a different church. Even though we don't see Riley any more, we know he's safe and happy in his new house with his family, right?"

Again, Amelia's head moved up and down. "Did our house burn down, Mama?" The question was almost a whisper and, not for the first time, Everly was slightly awed by how intuitive her daughter could be.

Kassandra Rennish had given Everly a truthful answer for Amelia, one she could understand. It was going to be hard no matter what, but at least a fire was something Amelia had a point of reference for.

She'd save the details of the many changes coming their way for another conversation. "It did, baby girl. I'm so sorry. But…" Before the words could actually sink in for Amelia, Everly eased her away and looked into her tear-glistening brown eyes. "But here's the good thing."

"Good thing?" Amelia sniffed. It was clear she was trying to be brave.

How she wished her daughter wouldn't swallow her emotions, but Everly understood. "We were going to move to a new house anyway, so friends of Mommy's packed up a bunch of our stuff and moved it. When we get to our new place, you'll see many of your things got there ahead of you."

"Mr. Ursa?"

Everly wasn't certain, but she didn't want to hurt her daughter any more than she already had. Besides, Mr. Ursa had come from the gift shop at one of the parks. Hopefully she could obtain another if the worst had happened. "I feel like he'll be there."

Amelia nodded again, then threw herself against her mother's chest and cried.

Jackson had never wanted so much to hold someone close.

Isaac and Freddy were due to arrive in a couple of hours, and that couldn't come fast enough. Jackson was exhausted and rapidly losing his grip on his emotions.

Watching from the kitchen, he rooted his feet to the floor. This was his fault. He should have been paying attention to the signs. Should have known Rennish and her handful of hangers-on would be vindictive.

No, this went back further. When Lance Carnalle died, Jackson should have stood his ground. Should have seen the truth that now smacked him in the chest so hard he almost lost his breath. If he had, he'd have stood by Everly and Amelia and the others in his care and might have seen this coming.

He'd let himself take on someone else's error. Lance Carnalle had made a choice Jackson had warned him against repeatedly. While Jackson could have stuck closer to him, Carnalle would have ultimately made the same decision at another time.

And had he turned all of his attention to Carnalle, he'd have pulled his attention from others.

Like the two sitting before him. If he'd stayed with the service, maybe he would have seen this coming.

But he hadn't. In his fit of pride and anger after Carnalle's murder, he'd run away and left Everly to someone else's care. Deputy Marshal Anderson had been a competent man, certainly, but Jackson had still failed to do what he'd known all along God was calling him to do.

Ruby had been right when they'd talked at Everly's friend's house. He was too self-focused and too job-focused.

As Everly held her daughter close and whispered quietly into the little girl's dark hair, the fire inside Jackson grew. They needed to be protected.

And Ruby was only half-right. Jackson's focus might be too much on himself, but it was clearly not enough on the job. He was missing details, and that had to stop.

Quietly, he motioned to Rex, who rested on his bed near the couch. Stepping out onto the front porch, he scanned the woods near the house as Rex sat expectantly beside him.

The yard was small, leaving enough outdoor space for only a small firepit near the front door. The cabin was well hidden among the trees, but that made it hard to see if anyone was sneaking up on them. Was this the ideal position or was it the most foolish one they could take, leaving themselves with no vision until danger was right on top of them?

He had been trained for witness security. The better course of action might have been to pack up Everly and Amelia and to head back to DC with himself as their protector instead of hanging around the area waiting for a handoff or another attempt on their lives.

Jackson laid his hand on the phone tucked securely in a zippered leg pocket. Maybe he should float that idea.

Or maybe he should stick to the plan.

He hated second-guessing himself. Usually he made a decision and ran with it, following protocol and procedures.

Right now, though, he was nothing like his usual self.

Dropping his hand to his side, he looked over his shoulder at the heavy log door. He was off his game because Everly was involved. There was something bigger going on between them than there ever should be. There had always been something bigger when it came to her.

He winced. Four years ago, he hadn't fully realized the dangerous line he was walking when it came to Everly Lopez. He'd known they were growing too close to one another.

He hadn't realized then just how deeply she'd made inroads into his heart.

Nearly kissing her last night had been a mistake. Letting himself pretend for even a moment that anything emotional could happen between them was utterly foolish.

Even though his heart wanted it all in the worst of ways.

This was a rookie mistake, one he'd have to fight if he wanted to protect Everly and get her and Amelia to safety. If he kept letting his emotions steal his focus, he'd lose them both forever.

He scanned the blue sky through the web of trees above him. He was going to lose them forever either way, once they disappeared into the system again. But at least if he kept his head in the game, they'd survive to live their lives, even though he wouldn't be part of those lives.

Behind him, the door creaked open. "Jackson?"

At the sound of Everly's near whisper, he steeled his

spine and stepped sideways to give her room to step onto the narrow porch. The family who had built the house had placed a small stoop on the forest side, choosing to concentrate their resources on a deck that faced the stunning views at the rear of the house.

It made for a cramped space with two people standing on the porch, crowded even more uncomfortably by the realizations he was wrestling.

Maybe if he didn't look at her... "How's Amelia?" He addressed the trees that waved gently in the breeze blowing over their heads from the lake.

"She cried for a bit, but I'm not sure how much she really understands. I think a lot of the tears had more to do with exhaustion and not fully understanding what's happening than with losing her home."

"Makes sense. There's been a lot of whiplash in her little life for the past couple of days."

"Mine, too." The words were a whisper, but they made their way past Jackson's stiff spine and into his soft heart.

He shouldn't hold her again.

Turning to her, he pulled her tightly to him and held her anyway. If he could just keep her here, sheltered and safe, then they could have all of the things he was coming to realize he wanted. Everly as his own. A home. A family.

"I'm scared." Her words muffled against his bicep, but they were loud and clear to the parts of his heart that cared more about her than he ever should. "I'm... angry. I'm...completely numb."

Jackson tipped his chin down and spoke into her hair. "You need some rest. Real rest." Exhaustion was rapidly claiming her ability to think rationally and to feel anything. "You're safe here. Dylan and I are watching. I'll be in the house and he'll be out here with Ridge. Take this time to heal a little. To let your brain stop thinking. To be in the moment." It was the kind of advice the counselors at WITSEC had often given to witnesses who were overwhelmed by the rapid changes in their lives, by the loss of purpose and identity. By the danger.

"In the moment?" Everly pulled back until she'd opened several inches of space between them. But she didn't back fully out of his arms nor pull her hands away from where they rested against his chest.

When she lifted her head and met his eyes, she was bound to be able to feel the change in his pulse rate, because her palms were over his heart, warm and exactly right.

He wanted to look away. He ought to look away.

But Everly here like this was perfect. In the moment, she was everything he wanted and she made him forget every resolution he'd just made.

She slipped her hands up and let them rest at the back of his neck, pulling him down toward her gently. She wanted the kiss they'd denied one another last night.

And so did he. Because it meant they were more than the friends he'd proclaimed they were.

Which was exactly wrong.

She had confessed she wasn't feeling anything. Everly was numb and looking for anything to make a connection. Right or wrong, it couldn't be Jackson.

Closing his eyes, he tilted his chin up, hoping that would be enough to signal the *no* he couldn't bring himself to say.

Everly stiffened, then dropped her arms and stepped

away. She turned to face the forest, her hands shoved into the pockets of her jeans.

He ought to be relieved. Instead he felt the chill of her removal and the disappointment of denial.

It was the thing that had to be done, though. This wasn't about him. This was fully about keeping her away from Kassandra Rennish and certain death.

Jackson mimicked her posture, their shoulders inches apart, giving her space. If he was honest, giving himself space as well.

Finally, she sighed. "This?" Pulling her hand from her pocket, she gestured toward the trees. "This is prime bear territory."

"How do you know?" She was choosing to talk about something neutral, and he'd let her.

She shrugged. "Instinct, in part. The lay of the land. The trees. The lake as a water and food source." She pointed to the right, where the forest sloped upward on a hillside. "I'm guessing if you were to cut through the underbrush and hike that way, you'd find several places suitable for hibernation." Her hand swung to the left, in front of Jackson, though she was clearly careful not to touch him. "If you look in the underbrush over there, you can see an animal trail that winds down to the river. I'm going to say there's deer here. Some cougar. Definitely bear. Maybe one will wander through our little clearing."

"I hope not." While he was familiar with the area and trained for every contingency, he'd never been fully comfortable with wildlife. Like people, they could be unpredictable and deadly.

"The more you know about them, the less scary they are." She dropped her hand. "Though I still wouldn't want to get between a mama and her cubs. Especially now, since I used up all of my bear spray and then gave my holster to Ruby."

"I noticed."

She shrugged again, her gaze never leaving the trees. "I won't need it wherever we end up."

"I'm sorry."

"All of this is hard." She leaned heavily against the rough-hewn porch post, still watching the forest. "I was one semester away from completing my doctorate. I had a job lined up with the Department of Fish and Wildlife. I was going to help educate the public and preserve wildlife habitats. Now?" She shrugged. "I have nothing. No matter how passionate I was about big animals in Texas, no matter how passionate I am about these wilderness creatures now... None of it matters." She gave a bitter chuckle. "The only constants in my life are Amelia and you."

He flinched. She didn't need to say things like that. "And God."

"I'm not talking to Him at the moment."

While he wanted to correct her, he let the comment lie. Her anger was normal and didn't need to be denied or smoothed over.

But Jackson as a constant? She couldn't continue to believe that. "I can't be someone you lean on." No matter how much he wanted to be.

"If I don't have you..." She let her voice trail off.

Man, how he wanted to pull her back against him. To reassure her and to make her a million promises.

Promises he'd have to break.

"You know this can't last. You're about to disappear

into another life, and I can't follow you." Although he wanted to do that more with each passing minute.

"I can't—"

"Jackson?" From the left, Dylan and Ridge jogged through the trees.

With a last glance at Everly, Jackson stepped down from the porch to meet them. "What's wrong?"

"I just got a call from the chief." Dylan's face was stony. He shot a quick look at Everly, then turned back to Jackson as Ridge heeled beside him. "We have a problem."

TWELVE

Reaching behind her, Everly grabbed the rough wooden post that supported the porch. It had supported this cabin for over a century, so it had to be strong enough to hold her up as well.

Although, with the weight Dylan's pronouncement had dropped into her chest, she might bring down the entire house and break through the wooden floor planks into the ground.

Jackson met Dylan at the foot of the steps. "What's going on?" His voice had changed, shifting from the quiet, almost gentle tone he'd used with her to one that projected. One that meant business.

Flicking a glance at Everly, Dylan shook his head once. Whatever it was, he didn't want her to hear.

It involved her. So far she'd been shut down, kept out of the loop and denied the opportunity to save herself.

That look snapped the last reserve she had.

"No." Shoving away from the post, she strode down the steps and slipped into the small space between Dylan and Jackson, her back nearly pressed to Jackson's chest and her nose aimed at Dylan's chin. She didn't care about personal space. They were going to hear her. "This is my life. You don't get to keep me out of it."

Surprisingly, Dylan took a step back, his mouth still clamped shut.

Well, Everly knew how this worked. As the lead on this entire makeshift team they'd put together to protect her, Jackson was the one in charge. He called the shots. If he ordered Dylan to tell her what had happened to put her life and her daughter's life into deeper jeopardy, then Dylan would have no choice.

She whirled on Jackson and lifted her chin to capture his gaze.

He stared over her head at Dylan.

If this was middle school, she'd punch him in the arm the way she used to slug her cousin when he wouldn't give up the baseball during her turn to pitch in their neighborhood pickup games. "I deserve to know."

Some sort of wordless communication passed between the two K-9 officers. Throughout the tautly stretched silence, Jackson never acknowledged she'd spoken. He simply watched Dylan as though he could read the news in the air between them.

It took a moment, but she felt the shift in Dylan's posture, as though he'd heard whatever Jackson wasn't saying loud and clear. "I got a call from the chief."

Even Everly knew that was never a good thing, not unless he was calling with news of Kassandra Rennish's apprehension. Given the air of dread around Dylan, it definitely wasn't that.

She turned slowly, fighting the urge to back up a step and lean against Jackson. She tried to will herself not to blush over the fact she'd practically thrown herself at him on the porch. He'd been right to step away.

Still, she wished he hadn't. It was wrong to make him the rock in her world. That put too much pressure on him and placed him on a pedestal no man deserved to occupy. While he could provide her with a bandage, he couldn't take care of the root of the trauma that now left her feeling nothing but numb.

Actually, that wasn't quite right. She wasn't entirely numb. The love for her daughter hadn't dimmed.

And her feelings for Jackson Dean were growing stronger with every moment they spent together. Going back into hiding forever as a new person was becoming a more difficult thought to deal with every second she spent with him.

Shaking her head to hopefully bring rational thinking back online, Everly focused on Dylan, who seemed to realize her mind had wandered somewhere far away.

But it was Jackson who spoke. "Is this about the decoy safe house?"

Dylan nodded. "It was shot up about half an hour ago."

The world seemed to tilt. Everly widened her stance to keep from tipping over.

Jackson rested a hand on her back almost as though he realized her balance had been rocked. "Our people?" His voice was clipped.

"Safe. They were there, but no one was hurt. They're still hunkered down inside, and an investigative team is en route, but they believe the shooter is gone."

"How did it happen?" Jackson stepped to her side, letting his hand slide to her shoulder. He pulled her against him as he tried to make sense of the danger.

It seemed as though the violence was escalating.

As though he could sense her fear, Rex moved from his position at Jackson's left side and walked around to sit by her, resting his shoulder against her leg.

Absently, she reached down and scratched behind his ear.

Dylan dragged his hand down his face. "The cabin they're at is in a clearing, with everything laid out similarly to the one we were in last night. Two gunmen set up shop on the perimeter after a sweep, one at the front and one at the back. They let loose with what appears to be some high-powered rifles and a few shotgun blasts for good measure."

Everly winced. From studying the methods both legal hunters and poachers used, she was well versed in the power of long guns. While rifles fired a single bullet, a well-placed shotgun blast would unleash the shrapnel of dozens of pellets. Birdshot wouldn't be a huge deal, but shells packed with larger pellets could do serious damage.

"There was no attempt to communicate?" Jackson's voice held a deadly tone.

"None."

There was silence between the men again, and Everly would give anything to know what wasn't being said. She opened her mouth to ask, but Dylan spoke first.

"There might be some good news, though." Dylan shifted tone. "The chief is talking to a contact he trusts with the Marshals, and he has a plan if they'll go for it."

It was as though a light bulb from the old cartoons popped on over Everly's head. For the first time, hope charged in, bolstered by the thoughts that started to race through her mind. "This could make Kassandra Rennish think I'm dead once and for all." If Jackson's K-9 unit and WITSEC could make it seem as though Everly had actually been inside the cabin and had been killed, then it might prevent the crime boss from searching for her again. She could finally stop looking over her shoulder.

"It's a possibility. Since Rennish sent the assassins, it won't look like a setup." Jackson's voice was thoughtful, though it still held a tinge of something heavy. "Even if it works, it won't change anything though."

Everly wished she could ignore the implications of his statement. He didn't simply mean it changed nothing for Everly. He meant it changed nothing for the two of them.

Everly and Amelia would still have to leave the area and move on with their lives under new identities. If they stayed, Rennish would eventually discover this had been a ruse and would come after them again.

The thought reignited the fire that had started burning in her the night before. "I mean it, Jackson." She turned and faced him, squaring off in the fight *of* her life…which was also the fight *for* her life. "I want to draw her out. You told me you think she's merely working with what little bit of an organization she has left. She's cruel enough to want to come after me on her own, just like…" Even all of these years later, she couldn't say it. The image of Noah taking his last breath while Kassandra Rennish gloated was the stuff of nightmares she'd never shake, no matter how much she healed emotionally or psychologically. If Kassandra had known Everly was upstairs…

Jackson reached for her as though he could read her thoughts, but she backed away. He didn't get to dictate what happened to her. He'd made it very clear he intended to keep his personal distance even though professionalism demanded he remain close.

When he moved to speak, Everly charged in to fill

the space with words before he could. "I want to put myself out there. I want more than for her to simply think I'm dead so I can start over somewhere else. I want to keep my life here. My child deserves better than to lose everything she knows."

"She's likely already lost everything." As Jackson spoke, Dylan gave Ridge a command and the pair slipped away around the corner of the cabin. "Your home is gone. You have nowhere to go back—"

"A house is one thing, but it's not the only thing that makes a life. We have friends. A church. A family not made of blood but of people who love us nonetheless." The wave of emotion that washed over her almost rocked her sideways again, but she stood her ground. "Beyond that..."

Her voice cracked, but she cleared her throat and charged ahead. He had to hear her. To understand her. She threw her arms out to the side. "Beyond that, Amelia has actual blood relatives who have never seen her. She has no idea her grandparents even exist. There are people who share her DNA who would move mountains for the chance to know her. And I..." She let her hands slap against her thighs as they fell. "I miss them."

She tried so hard not to think of her family or of Noah's parents. For all practical purposes, she was dead to them, and they were inaccessible to her. It was only in the dark nights when she couldn't sleep that the ache of wanting to feel her mother's hug or hear her father's laughter nearly swamped her. It was in those sleepless hours when she wondered what it would be like if they were present. How they'd spoil Amelia. What Christmases and birthdays would be like if they could all gather around the same table.

It took all of her strength to swallow the tears that threatened to crash a tidal wave over her arguments. "Jackson, I'm tired. I really don't think I have it in me to start over. I just… I want my life back. My actual, real, born-into-it life. I want to be the me I used to be. The *real* me."

There was more to it. So much more. It was clear Kassandra Rennish wanted her dead, and she didn't care who was caught in the cross fire.

She might want Everly dead or alive, but that "courtesy" didn't extend to Jackson. If Everly wanted to keep Jackson safe, then she needed to step up. Otherwise, Jackson could be killed while protecting her.

Everly couldn't survive if another man she cared about died at the hands of a murderer.

Everly didn't understand, and Jackson didn't want to explain it to her.

She was so fired up right now. So certain she could fix everything. So full of what his great-grandmother used to call "spit and vinegar…" Part of him wanted to let her rage on and fight this thing to the end. To let her hold on to the hope that there could be a good outcome that allowed her to live her own life again.

One that allowed her to be with him.

He wasn't sure if that was what was on her mind or in her heart, but it certainly kept rising in his chest with a hope that burned so hot it was a blue flame. If they could apprehend Kassandra Rennish and isolate her from the outside world, then maybe all of those things Jackson had never allowed himself to consider—

"No." The word blasted from his mouth as if it had been fired from one of the shotguns that had nearly killed two PNK9 agents today. Thankfully, Everly had no idea he was trying to silence his thoughts more than her words.

Everly physically jerked, stepping back from him as though the denial had punched her in the chest.

"No?" Oh, that word wasn't soft. It carried all of the violent fire of a volcano. She stepped closer with the glow of hot lava in her gaze. "It's. My. Life."

"And Amelia's." That ought to throw water on the fire. "Don't forget you're her only parent."

Everly's face turned red, and her eyes went wide. For a hot minute, it looked as though she was going to explode.

Just as suddenly, the starch in her posture vanished as her shoulders slumped. "You're right." She walked around him and sat on the porch steps, burying her face in her hands.

Jackson followed. He settled beside her but made sure to keep space between them. He'd already proven to himself he couldn't touch her without pushing past professional and into personal. He didn't need to make that mistake now when so much was on the line.

And so much was on the line. What Everly couldn't see was Kassandra Rennish had changed tactics. Her goons had peppered that cabin without concern for who was inside or what state their bodies might be in in the aftermath. There was no longer a "bring Everly Lopez to me dead or alive" order.

For Kassandra Rennish, Everly's death had become the only option. If Everly put herself out there as bait, they had no way to guarantee Rennish or one of her people wouldn't snipe her from a distance.

Everly raised her head and stared at the trees closest

to the cabin. "Sometimes I get so busy trying to save Amelia that I forget she needs me. I get a superhero complex or something."

"Understandable."

She tilted her head to look at him and then, just as quickly, she looked away. "I guess you understand. Probably a hazard of your job in law enforcement."

It was something many struggled with when they put on the uniform. Pride could grow into a mighty issue. That feeling of invincibility could magnify exponentially if it wasn't held in check. He'd seen more than one dangerous situation where, in the heat of the moment, someone with a badge rushed in, forgetting they were human.

He'd been to more than one funeral because of it.

As much as he tried to avoid that bulletproof mentality, there was no denying it could creep in on the best of officers. "It can be. Sometimes, with all of the training and with the fact we're the ones people call to protect them from danger, it's easy to forget we're susceptible to danger as well."

"I don't forget." Her brow furrowed. "About you, I mean. There's no dead or alive option when it comes to you. She'll kill you to get to me, without hesitating. She has no reason to spare you, especially if you're between her and me. And I know you. That's exactly where you'll be. It's your job."

True. But this had grown far beyond his job. The need to protect her and Amelia had taken root at some point in the hospital after Amelia was born. He hadn't realized it until today, but it had been growing ever since. Now it was as tall as some of the centuries-old trees that reached to the sky above them.

He had no idea how to curb the feelings, either. All he could do was hide them behind the job.

The job he should be doing instead of fighting daydreams about a future that could never exist. "We need to talk about something."

"There's more?" The words were flat. Despite her earlier bravado, it was clear exhaustion and overwhelming emotions had forced her into autopilot. "What don't I know?"

She might as well know everything. Maybe it would help her to be more cautious. "I think the dead or alive order on you has expired as well." He studied her profile, waiting to see the moment reality hit.

But her expression didn't change. "I know." She gave her head a quick shake, sending her hair into a slight sway. "There was no holding back when they shot up the cabin. It didn't matter to them who was killed. Whatever it is she wanted me alive for, it's out the window now."

Here was the thing he wanted to discuss. There was a reason Kassandra had wanted to look Everly in the eye…and there was also a reason she wanted her dead. This went beyond revenge. "What makes you a threat to her?"

Everly shrugged. "If I knew, I'd find a way to eliminate the threat."

"Understandable."

"She told me point-blank as she was leaving court she'd kill me if she had the chance. Now she's busted out of prison and she's coming at me with all she has. But to initially tell her crew she preferred me to be alive? I have no idea."

The wind off the lake picked up as the afternoon sun warmed the day, kicking the tall evergreens into a stirring dance. Jackson watched them wave against the piercing blue sky, considering all that had happened. "Kassandra went to jail for murdering Noah. She was never found guilty of any crimes related to her syndicate."

Everly pursed her lips. "When he died, his testimony died with him. He was the linchpin of the case the prosecution was building."

From the case files, he knew Kassandra hadn't yet been charged with any crimes when she murdered Noah. He had only recently gone to the FBI about her trafficking operation and was helping them during the evidence-gathering stage. Kassandra would likely have gotten away with his murder if Everly hadn't been upstairs to witness the killing. "Did Noah have any documents? Anything he was holding back?"

"I would have turned over anything if I'd had it or if I'd known where it was. All I knew was he was taking photographs and scanning documents to hand over, but I don't know how far he'd gotten. They never found his files."

"And Rennish's people long ago destroyed everything that could implicate her...or them."

Running her hands down her blue-jeaned thighs, Everly turned her face toward the sky. "I'm no threat to her."

"But she thinks you know something, and it's doubtful anything would convince her otherwise." For Rennish to risk her newly stolen freedom on a personal assault, there was something big on the line. Something bigger than revenge. "Noah never told you any details? Never mentioned where he might keep things he didn't want found until he was ready?"

"Never." Everly's sigh was heavy with the weight of the past five years. "We talked at length before he went to the authorities about the danger we could both be in. He told me a few reasons why he wanted to turn her in, human trafficking being the top of the list. Nothing he said to me would stand up in court, though, because it would all be hearsay, and there was nothing that could tear her down now if she wanted to rebuild. I knew a few generalities, enough for Noah to impress upon me the need for him to put our lives at risk, but he never gave me details. He never told me where he was hiding anything."

"She could think you have Noah's evidence. The fire at your house could have been more about destroying anything left behind than it was about causing you pain."

"Then she wasted a match." The words were bitter as anger bubbled back to the surface. "I still don't know why God would let this happen." Bracing her hands on her knees, Everly stood so abruptly that the cross charm on her necklace swung. "I know nothing that would cause Kassandra Rennish any harm. She needs to let it go." Stomping up the two steps, she entered the house, closing the door softly behind her.

Jackson winced as though she'd slammed it, because he had no doubt that was exactly what she'd have rather done. She'd never risk waking Amelia from a sleep free of the nightmare they were currently living in.

Standing, Jackson walked to the space where the driveway opened into the small clearing where the house stood. He stared for a long time at the narrow path that was covered in a thick layer of evergreen needles and was dark with the shadows of overhanging limbs. With their location essentially off the grid, they were relatively safe until WITSEC dealt with their issues and took Everly and Amelia out of his life for good.

Until then, it was his job to focus on keeping her safe. The ruse they were setting up at the other cabin had better work, because what Everly truly knew didn't matter. The issue was what Kassandra believed she knew...and there was no doubt the other woman wouldn't stop until she believed Everly was dead.

THIRTEEN

The sun drifted to the west, casting the lake and the waterfront side of the cabin into long shadows.

Everly stood in the kitchen, as far from the floor-to-ceiling windows as possible, staring out at the peaceful scene that did nothing to calm her nerves. Without window coverings, she felt exposed, as though a sniper rifle was trained on her every time she walked back and forth across the kitchen.

Jackson had said there was no way anyone could know where they were located and the odds of Kassandra Rennish having access to a sniper who could fire across the lake were pretty much nonexistent, but still… She had learned long ago not to trust conjecture. The only things she had faith in at the moment were the things her eyes could see.

Right now, all her eyes could see was a giant wall of windows that offered no place to hide.

Still staring at the vista in front of her, she stirred the small pot filled with jarred spaghetti sauce. Thankfully, whoever had sent food had landed on Amelia's favorite. They'd eaten their share of spaghetti over the years. The familiarity should help Amelia feel more at ease, but only if Everly could keep her from sensing the fear that seemed to roll off her in waves.

She tapped the spoon against the pot and laid it on the stove. Jackson had said Isaac was on the way, so she'd made enough for a small army to eat.

At the sound, Amelia looked up from coloring, but she went back to work without speaking. She'd been quiet since waking from her nap, and she hadn't been interested in snuggles like she often was.

Everly kept her distance. Sometimes Amelia liked to ponder things quietly. If Everly pushed, her daughter would lash out in a "hissy fit," as her grandmother liked to call them. Four-year-olds didn't process emotions like adults and couldn't always articulate their feelings, so Everly tried to understand those angry outbursts when they erupted.

But wouldn't throwing a "hissy fit" of her own feel amazing? Everly leaned against the counter. Anger had been building since she'd flamed up at Jackson in the driveway, holding at a simmer since. As she watched her daughter withdraw into coloring pages, the emotion threatened to blow.

Why, God? Everly dug her teeth into her lip to keep from saying the words aloud. If Kassandra Rennish hadn't orchestrated a jailbreak and come after her, then she'd be making spaghetti in her own cheery kitchen, with the red plaid curtains that added a pop of color to contrast with the creamy white cabinets she'd painted herself. Amelia would be chattering about her day with Tara and the kids while Everly cut up vegetables for a salad. After dinner, they'd clean up the kitchen together and then watch cartoons on one of the throwback streaming services until it was Amelia's bedtime.

Instead, Everly couldn't even guarantee they'd get to eat the spaghetti she was making in this borrowed cabin in this borrowed kitchen in this borrowed corner of the park she could only find on a map because she recognized the lake.

Noah had done the right thing. He'd wanted justice for the people Kassandra Rennish had been trafficking. He'd wanted stolen money restored to the families Kassandra had conned out of millions. But it had all been for nothing, because the evidence was gone… and so was Noah.

Everly had done the right thing as well, testifying to the horror she'd witnessed, wanting justice for her husband and to prevent Kassandra Rennish from harming anyone again.

Yet Kassandra had escaped. She'd murdered a federal agent. She'd injure or kill others in order to get to Everly.

How did I do the right things and yet I'm the one who's suffering the consequences? She hurled the silent question at the ceiling. *Jackson promised I could trust You. I have. I really have. But I've got nothing to show for it. Not even You.*

That was the worst part. She felt as though she'd lost the God she'd trusted, the One constant in her life. It seemed He was silent. That He didn't care. That He'd abandoned the plan for her life.

She'd laid everything out and—

"Mama, look!" The chair slid backward and almost crashed to the floor as Amelia rocketed from her seat, pointing to the side window into the dense forest near the house.

Everly's heart squeezed into her throat, choking off

her air. What was wrong? Did she call for Jackson? Scoop up Amelia and run? Try to defend—

"Bears, Mama." Amelia's voice dropped to a whisper and she moved slower, the way she'd been taught to do whenever wildlife was nearby. "Out the window."

With a resounding *thump* that seemed to shudder her muscles back into action, Everly's heart started beating again. She sagged against the counter. Bears. It was just bears.

With an impatient huff, Amelia waved her over. "You're going to miss them."

Steadying her voice so she could speak, Everly took a second to refocus her thoughts, then shoved away from the counter. "You're right. I don't want to miss this." Walking softly so as not to make excess noise that might frighten the wildlife, Everly approached her daughter and knelt beside her, wrapping one arm around her waist.

Outside the large windows, just inside the tree line, a mother bear and her months-old cub rooted around the edges of a rotted stump, likely distracted by the presence of ants or beetle larvae on their way to the lake below. A narrow, well-worn strip of dirt that wound through the trees indicated this was an often-used path the animals traveled to reach water.

Had she not been so distracted, she would have noticed it before.

Amelia turned to whisper directly into her mother's ear. "Can we get closer?"

The window was about ten feet from them, and the bears were about that far again from the cabin. They were likely safe in the house, but there was a good chance they'd scare the bears. Also, Everly wasn't really certain how much she trusted the giant panes of plate glass against an angry mama bear's considerable weight, no matter how thick and sturdy they seemed to be. "I think here is best. We don't want the mama to think we're trying to hurt her baby. She doesn't understand there's glass between us, and she doesn't know we only want to watch."

Nodding slowly, Amelia leaned against Everly, the warmth of her tiny body the greatest comfort Everly could imagine.

"What are they eating?"

Everly smiled at Amelia's whisper. Even from a distance and behind a wall of glass, she was concerned about disturbing the mama and her cub. It was one of those moments when Everly knew she'd taught her daughter something of value.

She gave Amelia a quick squeeze. "Bears like to eat all sorts of things. We've talked about this before. What do you remember?"

Amelia's face scrunched up. "Grass and…bugs. There's probably bugs in that tree stump." With a sigh of contentment, she leaned her head against her mother's. "God made sure the bears had plenty to eat."

The words jolted through Everly as though they'd come out of the air instead of from her daughter. "What did you say?"

"You told me. God makes sure the bears have food to eat and caves to sleep in and water to drink." She shrugged as though her words didn't carry the weight of the prayers Everly had been praying. "You said God takes care of them, and He takes care of us."

It was so simplistic, the things she'd said to her daughter during bedtime prayers or on rides home from church. Sure, the bears had food now, but there were forest fires, droughts, floods...

Floods like the recent ones that had swelled the river she'd been forced to jump into. The river that was usually so shallow she'd have broken her back on any other day.

Floods also filled up lakes and reservoirs, providing water for months and years.

Fires caused devastating destruction, but they also allowed nature the space to renew and regrow.

There was a Bible verse somewhere about beauty out of ashes.

It was all too simplistic. Too...easy.

As the mama and her cub lumbered off toward the lake, Amelia extracted herself from Everly's arms and went back to her artwork.

But Everly stayed where she was, on her knees, staring at the breeze-tossed trees.

Truth could sometimes be simple, but that didn't make it easy. Life held hard truths, as she'd learned well. Questions weren't always answered, or they offered answers no one wanted to hear.

If the aftermath of a forest fire brought renewed life, something that could be turned into good in the long term, then couldn't life work that way as well?

The pain of loss didn't go away just because strength or purpose came later. And tragedies were still tragedies, even when there were silver linings to pin hope onto. People still lost homes or died along with animals in fires or floods or droughts. Those things were unthinkably tragic and awful and heavy.

But there was always new growth behind the fires

and floods. Beauty from the ashes. But only if she looked beyond today and the midst of the pain.

As Jackson had told her during their talks in the hospital, today and this life weren't all she had. If she believed in Jesus, there was so much more beyond today. There was a bigger picture she'd never understand, and that was the thing that required faith. Even when nothing made sense, faith believed God saw the bigger, longer picture and was taking care of her in that long view, even though the present was a falling-apart, horrid, terrifying mess.

Everly dropped her chin to her chest and closed her eyes. The anger didn't die. Her questions didn't go away. But peace seemed to cover everything like a blanket, smothering some of the flames so she could deal with the embers later, when her emotions weren't so fragile.

The floor behind her creaked and Jackson crouched beside her.

Although she hadn't heard him come into the house, his presence didn't surprise her. He leaned his shoulder against hers as Rex trotted up and sat pressed against her other side.

"Why are we sitting on the floor?" Jackson's voice was barely audible over Rex's panting.

As though she'd heard him, Amelia leaped from her chair. "There were bears, Mr. Jack!"

"Bears?" He addressed Everly, but there was a different question in his expression, one that asked if she was okay.

Now wasn't the time to get into what was happening in her heart and mind. It was too fresh. Too much something she needed to spend quiet time addressing with God first. She simply gave him a quick nod with what she hoped looked like a gentle smile. "A mama and her cub. They headed toward the lake."

"The baby was cute, Mr. Jack! Come look out the window, maybe we can see them at the water."

Jackson stood and went to Amelia, but Rex stayed pressed against Everly's side as though he could tell she needed something she couldn't articulate.

Everly laid a hand on the Doberman's head and scratched his ear. In vet school years ago, she'd learned rubbing a dog's ears released endorphins, and Rex leaned into the attention as though he felt every one of the molecules releasing in his brain.

This time, Everly's smile was real. Maybe Rex's good feelings were transferring to her, but more likely, God was already working at healing the deepest parts of her heart.

She was still in the middle of the fight for her life, but no matter what happened…

She was going to survive.

Amelia dried the last plate and handed it to Jackson. "All done."

Jackson had volunteered himself and Amelia to do dishes while Dylan patrolled and Everly had some much-needed quiet time.

He had a feeling something had happened to her after their bear sighting. At dinner, she'd been quiet but seemingly at peace. When she'd asked for a few minutes to herself, Jackson had readily agreed. She deserved it, having been on the move nonstop for over twenty-four hours. As a single mom, her alone time was probably pretty rare.

"Mr. Jack?" Amelia poked him in the stomach and held out the plate. "Do you want to put this away?"

He'd washed, Amelia had dried, and he'd tucked away the dishes in the overhead cabinets, stepping over Rex, who lay on the floor hoping to catch some crumbs.

Jackson was impressed with Amelia's helpful attitude. Her mother had raised her well. "How about you put this one away?" Jackson took the plate and looked down at the little girl with the same big brown eyes that had captured his heart four years earlier. It was hard to believe she was the tiny baby he'd been terrified of breaking. Babies were small to begin with, but Amelia's low weight due to her premature birth had made Jackson feel like a fumbling giant.

Somehow he'd managed to keep her safe. From the moment he'd first held her, he'd vowed to protect her and her mother.

Now, looking down at her bright eyes, he doubled down on that vow.

Those eyes almost disappeared in a skeptical squint. The cabinets were above the counter, far above Amelia's head. "Mama says I can't climb on the counters."

"That's a good rule, but Mama didn't say anything about learning to fly."

Her eyebrows knit together with questions, and her face scrunched around her nose. She planted her hands on her hips, the dish towel she clasped hanging nearly to the floor. "You know people can't fly, right?"

She looked so much like a mother who was scolding her rambunctious children that Jackson had to force a laugh down into a chuckle to keep her from thinking he was making fun of her. He cleared his throat. "I'm sure you can."

Her chin dipped, and she looked up at him through long eyelashes.

Before she could argue again, he slid the plate onto the counter and scooped her up. She was so light he nearly tossed her through the log roof.

Amelia giggled wildly. "Higher!"

Lofting her to shoulder height, Jackson shifted until he held her straight out like she was flying, bracing her under the chest and above her knees. He swooped her toward the counter.

Rex jumped up and barked once, joining in on the fun.

Amelia grabbed the plate and slid it into place when Jackson swooped her higher. Slamming the cabinet door, she giggled. "Done! Fly me to the window!"

"As you wish." Whirling, Jackson headed for the window as quickly as he safely could with the little girl in his arms and his partner racing ahead to lead the way. He slowed and gently tapped her forehead against the glass. "Sorry, little bird. We can't go any further."

She whipped her head around to look at him, and he had to scramble to keep his grip on her. Her eyes were fiery, like her mother's could be. "I am *not* a bird."

"You're not? But you can fly."

If she could have planted her hands on her hips, she probably would have. "I'm a superhero."

Jackson nearly snorted. "Oh, excuse me."

"Yeah, we're all about superheroes in the Lopez household." Everly's voice drifted from behind.

Holding Amelia in full flight position, Jackson turned. "I'm an action movie guy myself."

"Not surprising." Everly stood with her shoulder leaning against the doorway of the short hallway that led to the two bedrooms. With the slight, easy smile on her face, she looked every inch the doting mother laughing at the antics of father and daughter.

The joy leaked straight out of Jackson, through his feet to the plank floor. This wasn't his family. Everly wasn't his wife.

And Amelia was not his daughter.

Gently, he settled Amelia onto the floor, and Rex sat beside her protectively.

Here came that look again, the same narrow-eyed chastisement he'd received in the kitchen. "Mr. Jack, I wasn't done flying."

Neither was he, but he couldn't keep up the fun. He needed his feet planted firmly on the ground if he was going to stay true to the vow he'd made only moments before. "Sorry, kiddo. I'm not as strong as a superhero is. I need to take a rest."

Amelia nodded wisely, as though the explanation made perfect sense. "What now, though?"

Clearly, she wanted to continue the game but, while Jackson knew how to start the fun, he wasn't exactly sure how to make it stop without crushing the little girl's enthusiasm.

"Okay, my little flying squirrel." Everly straightened and walked toward them, stopping at the back of the couch. "It's time for you to take a shower. You managed to get out of having one last night, but you're going to get the funk if you skip another day."

It seemed as though Amelia might argue, but Everly had perfected the universal "you'd better get moving" mom look. A quick view of that set the little girl into motion, but she stopped a few feet from Jackson and looked back, lowering her chin and her voice. "We'll fly more later. After you rest." She zoomed off before he could respond.

Everly tapped her daughter on the head as she passed. "Tara packed you some shampoo. It's in the shower. I put a towel in there and I'll bring you some pj's. The water turns on just like ours at home. Call me if you need help."

"Yes, ma'am!" Amelia saluted and zoomed through the door, disappearing from view.

Everly rolled her eyes. "Tara introduced her to a ton of those superhero movies last year. I've heard about very little else since then."

"There are worse things she could obsess over."

"True." Everly braced her hands on the back of the couch, watching him. "Amelia likes you. It won't be easy when you're gone again." There was no censure, just truth.

It would be hard on Jackson, too. The longer he was with them, the more thoughts of them taking up permanent residence in his life intruded.

That was something he couldn't have. He had no serious relationship with Everly, no claims to her future, no matter how close they once were or had become. There was no guarantee they'd spend their lives together if he went into hiding with them. He could sacrifice everything and end up with nothing. It didn't feel like the right thing to do.

Besides, he'd have to give up his law enforcement career to go with them. He knew his calling was "to protect and serve." To do anything different would be to deny everything God had ever told him.

This was one of those "deny yourself, take up your cross and follow Me" moments. He'd thought he knew all about sacrifice due to his career, but personal sacrifice? That was completely different.

He forced himself to look her in the eye, then shifted his gaze to watch her run her finger along the back of the couch, a nervous gesture she didn't seem to realize she was doing. "It's a hard, weird situation for all of us, I think."

"I'm pretty sure no one else in the world is facing one like it." Everly lifted a smile that, while sad, held some measure of the peace he'd noticed earlier.

"You seem more relaxed."

The restless fiddling with the couch seam stopped, and her smile brightened. "I had a chat with God. While I'm not okay with what's happening, I'm…" She pursed her lips and stared out the window behind Jackson. "I'm choosing to trust Him. I'm fighting to do it, and the level of trust changes every second, but I'm choosing to do it."

Jackson nodded. *Good.* That was what she needed to do. "I think—"

"Mama! I can't make the water work!"

Everly's eyebrows shot up and down quickly, like they'd bounced with amusement. "I knew that was coming." She turned toward the hallway door, then stopped to look back. "I'll probably help her and then lie down with her until she falls asleep. Then I'll probably drop off, too. But I wanted to say, well…thank you."

Before Jackson could respond, she disappeared into the shadows of the short hallway.

She was more welcome than she knew.

He waited until he heard the bedroom door close, then turned to look out the panoramic windows. With night only an hour or so away, it was probably best if

Everly and Amelia stayed out of sight in the bedroom. While he didn't think anyone knew where they were, he wasn't a fan of the wide-open view into the cabin from the lake.

With a sigh, he turned away and glanced over the living area, strewn with evidence a child had taken over the space. The team had gone all out sending toys and art supplies. Amelia probably thought it was Christmas.

He ought to get outside and take a few hours of perimeter patrol so Dylan and Ridge could rest, speaking of the team.

There were no stairs from the ground up to the deck, so he wasn't concerned with anyone making their way into the house other than through the front door. He could safely leave Amelia and Everly inside while he stepped out to meet Dylan. He pulled his phone out and dashed off a quick text. Meet me at the front porch. You need a break. Dylan would call to confirm, per the chief.

With a snap of his fingers, he called Rex from the window and headed for the door, retrieving his sidearm from a locked box on top of the fridge.

His phone chimed, but it wasn't Dylan. The text from the chief pressed Pause on the world. WITSEC en route to pick up witness. Escorted by Danica. ETA 2100.

He made a quick call for verbal confirmation of the intel, then slid his phone into his pocket and stepped outside. The approaching sunset brought cooler temperatures, but it didn't really matter.

His time with Everly was over. He ought to tell her, but first he needed a moment to get his emotions in check. Taking a few laps around the perimeter with Rex would help, but where was Dylan?

Jackson commanded Rex to sit, then scanned the trees.

Silence.

Jackson's jaw tightened. The area around the cabin was small, so Dylan couldn't have gone far. Reaching back to lock the dead bolt with the key, he stepped off the porch. If Dylan doubled back, he had the other key.

He texted again. Status?

No response.

Something was wrong. Jackson looked down at Rex. He could leave his partner behind to stand guard, but, to avoid dangerous misunderstandings, he was trained to protect or attack only on command.

He had no choice. Everly and Amelia should be safe inside the locked cabin for a few minutes.

With Rex at his side, Jackson walked toward the vehicles, scanning the ground for footprints.

A rustling to his right sent his hand to his Sig. He stepped behind the shelter of his SUV as the sound came closer.

Ridge emerged from the woods at a full run, dropping to sit in front of Jackson and panting heavily.

Jackson knelt in front of the K-9.

The Saint Bernard's black vest was smeared with blood.

FOURTEEN

Everly sat on the edge of the bed and exhaled, basking in newfound peace. Steam rolled through the bathroom door that stood half-open so she could listen to Amelia as she showered and sang a song about a big red car.

Smiling, Everly stood and went to the backpack on the antique pine chest of drawers. Someday she'd have to find a way to thank Tara for the old portable CD player and stack of early 2000s kiddie music. Amelia's musical tastes might never be the same.

Sadness crept in, overlaying her peace like a thundercloud covering the sun. The chances she'd ever get to relay a message to Tara were less than zero, but maybe she could pass along a note through Jackson before they parted ways.

That was another thing she didn't want to think about. *Lord, I need that peace back, please.* She stopped with her fingertips pressed onto the top of the chest of drawers. "And thank You for it in the first place." The whispered words edged a few of the dark clouds away. Somehow, it would all work out the way it was supposed to, even if that way wasn't what she'd have wanted or asked for.

"Dylan!" Jackson's voice came through the house from somewhere near the porch.

Everly froze. Typically, the two of them texted back and forth instead of advertising their presence. Her heartbeat picked up against her rib cage. She eased toward the window, peeking through the curtains toward the front stoop, the corner of which she could just make out from her angle.

Silence.

Nothing seemed to be out of place. A few bushes snapped back and forth as though someone had just passed through them, and a shadow moved away from the house.

Everly twisted her lips and watched. Likely, Jackson had seen the other officer and had hailed him instead of texting, and they were patrolling together before nightfall.

When nothing else happened, she backed away from the window. If something was wrong, he'd have told her.

Fighting an uneasy roll in her stomach, Everly grabbed the last clean pair of pajamas from Amelia's backpack and headed back to the bathroom. Hopefully there was a laundry room tucked somewhere in this cabin, or she'd be washing dirty clothes in the sink after Amelia went to bed.

Shoving the bathroom door fully open, she stopped to let the excess steam escape. Ever since Amelia had shifted from baths to showers, she'd insisted on the warmest water and the longest shower. The water bill would be insane by the time that girl was a teenager, no matter where they lived.

Hopefully, not in an area prone to drought.

From the shower, Amelia moved on loudly to a song about hot potatoes and cold spaghetti.

Yep, she'd have to thank Tara for the brand-new ear-worms…somehow. Everly shoved aside a tube of toothpaste to lay the pajamas on the narrow counter. "When you get out, dry off and put on your pj's. I'll be at the kitchen table."

The song broke off. "Okay, Mama." Without missing a beat, Amelia went on to a new verse about mashed bananas.

Clearly, she'd be a while…and Everly would let her. She wanted to spend some time with the small waterproof Bible she kept tucked into her backpack. She just needed concrete words. One corner of the kitchen table was tucked out of sight from the large windows. Maybe, while Amelia was occupied and Jackson was outside, she could find enough peace to not just carry her through the night but on into this new season she was facing.

The sun had nearly dropped below the horizon when she walked out of the short hallway into the living area. Full dark would come soon. She folded her arms, pressing the Bible tightly against her stomach. The room in front of her was so exposed. She'd retreat to the bedroom as soon as Jackson and Rex or Dylan and Ridge came in.

Even with the peace she now felt about her circumstances, she couldn't seem to come to any sort of sense of reconciliation where Jackson was concerned. Every minute she spent in his presence, she wanted to pile on more minutes, more hours, more days…

Everly leaned against the narrow wall between the

bedroom hallway and the hall that ran along the kitchen to the front door.

It had been years since she'd felt this way. The grief over losing Noah and then finding out she carried their child had brought her to her knees in ways she'd never thought possible. She'd been certain her heart was shattered and she'd never be capable of loving again.

But then Amelia had been born. Holding her baby girl in her arms and basking in her tiny, precious presence had healed so many of Everly's broken places.

Befriending Jackson had healed more. He'd been exactly what she and Amelia had both needed in those dark days.

When Jackson had woven Jesus through every conversation, Everly had realized how real He was and how much she wanted Him in her life. That was when healing had moved toward completion.

The deep wounds were scars that still burned at times, but over the years, God had knit her heart together again. The grief of missing Noah still coursed through her with an ache she could feel at times, but being around Jackson again made one thing clear.

She had a full heart that was ready to love again.

Unfortunately, the man her heart had softened toward was the man she couldn't have. She'd never ask him to give up his life and his career to hide with her in some unknown corner of the country, where he could never serve in law enforcement again. It would be selfish of her.

She'd have to deal all over again with her heart being ripped in two.

The more she stayed out of his way now, the easier it would be to say goodbye when the time came.

Thinking about that unraveled her peace, so she pushed that thought aside. For now, she'd hide in the corner, out of sight.

Shoving away from the wall, Everly took two steps, glancing toward the front door before she slowed and stopped, her hands falling to her sides.

The heavy wooden door was open slightly, as though it hadn't been closed all the way.

Everly's fingers dug into the heavy plastic cover on her small Bible. There was no way Jackson would have stepped away without securing the door.

Everly crept forward, eyes on the slight opening as though a creature might leap through at any second. Not daring to peek out, she pushed the door shut and turned the dead bolt. Jackson and Dylan had keys. They'd be able to—

Something rustled behind her.

Cold metal pressed against the base of her skull, shoving her head into the doorway. A hand pressed into the center of her back, jolting her forward as the Bible fell to the floor.

"If you want me to leave your daughter safely where she is, you'll come with me quietly."

A low-hanging limb crashed against Jackson's shoulder as he barreled through the trees, knocking his right half sideways and tweaking something in his spine. Pain arced through his muscles, but he tried to ignore the white heat of it, following Ridge. Rex was close on his heels. Lower to the ground, the K-9s didn't have to deal with the branches and bushes that hindered Jackson on the nearly overgrown animal trail.

He glanced back toward the cabin, now out of sight

through the trees. Surely Everly and Amelia would be safe for a few minutes. The greater threat was to Dylan, if that was his blood on Ridge's vest.

He prayed it wasn't.

He resisted calling for his teammate again, drawing his sidearm as he followed Ridge deeper into the forest. As a clearing opened up ahead of them, he slowed, gesturing for Rex to stay behind him as he crept closer.

In the middle of the open space, Dylan was struggling to sit up. He'd rolled onto his side and was pushing himself from the ground.

"Stay down." Jackson scanned the trees around the clearing, which was barely more than an opening in the trail. If anyone was hiding out there waiting to take them down, they were well concealed.

He glanced back at Rex, who watched him carefully for a command. He showed no signs of alerting on anyone else's presence or of sniffing at the air with interest. Neither did Ridge.

Dropping to his knees beside Dylan, Jackson holstered his Sig and helped his teammate sit up. Rex and Ridge sat at Dylan's other side. "What happened?"

"Not sure." Touching the back of his head, Dylan winced when he drew his fingers away and saw blood. "It wasn't a hard hit, but it was enough to put me on my knees."

Jackson jerked his head down in a silent command, and Dylan obeyed, letting Jackson inspect the wound. "Looks superficial. Lots of cuts and scrapes. Nothing that looks like stitches. Did it knock you out?" If Dylan had been unconscious, even for a moment, then they had bigger problems on their hands.

"No. Just stunned me. It came out of nowhere. They

caught me in the head, then in my back once I was face-down. It took the wind out of my lungs. I thought I was done, but... It was weird. They knelt over me like they were going to finish the job, then they didn't."

Rocking back on his heels, Jackson scanned the woods. Whoever had found them, they were being careful. Leaving a trail of too many bodies would only add to their legal troubles if they were caught. It was clear they had the single-minded mission of getting to Everly and dealing with her. Killing another law enforcement officer was secondary if they could reach Everly without the added bloodshed.

Either that, or Everly's would-be killer wanted her protectors to suffer in their failures if she was killed. That was a cruel fate, worse than death for those who'd sworn to protect and serve.

He should know.

He shook off his past mistakes and left them on the forest floor, the way Everly had urged him to. Living in another man's death wasn't going to rescue her today. "You okay to move?" The timing wasn't ideal, but they needed to get back to the cabin.

"I'm fine." Dylan shrugged off Jackson's help and stood. "Somebody's here. This could be the final showdown."

No need to tell him twice. In his mind, Jackson was already halfway up the path back to Everly. "We've got backup coming. Isaac should be here at any second, and WITSEC is coming with Danica in a couple of hours." Until then, it was only the two of them and their partners on deck. "Let's get moving."

He led the way up the narrow animal trail, still rushing but not as heedlessly this time. His back still throbbed from the torquing it had taken when he whacked that tree branch. If he injured himself, he would be no help to Everly or Amelia.

He needed to get to them, to make sure whoever had injured Dylan and had lured them both away from the house hadn't already reached them. "I locked the door when I came after you. I'll go inside and check on Everly and her daughter. You—"

"Jack?" Dylan had stopped in the middle of the trail. When Jackson turned, he was checking his pockets. "My key's gone." He stopped his frantic search and lifted his gaze to Jackson's. "They weren't trying to kill me. They knew I had a key."

Whirling, Jackson broke into a run, recklessly dodging branches. Rex followed closely. If someone knew exactly where Dylan had stashed his key to the house, then they'd been watching for some time. They'd seen him lock the door and had taken note of which pocket he'd slipped the key into.

They'd never been safe here. Kassandra Rennish had always known where to find them. The shoot-out at the other house had been a decoy to lull them into a false sense of security.

They'd all fallen for it.

A shriek shattered the twilight. "Mama!" Amelia's frantic voice raced through the trees and dug claws into his heart. "Mama! Mr. Jack! Rex!" Her shouts were ragged with terror.

Jackson ran harder, bursting into the clearing on the echoes of Amelia's cries.

The little girl stood in the doorway to the cabin, dressed in pajamas dotted with horses and flowers. Wet hair tangled around her face and tears streaked her cheeks. As soon as she saw Jackson, she exploded off the porch in her bare feet, launching herself at him the moment he drew near.

He hefted her and held her close, her face buried in his neck, tears wetting his skin. She was hysterical. There would be no information from her until he calmed her down.

He strode to the porch and sat on the top step, cradling the little girl against his chest and trying to quiet her sobs even as his own heart raced with adrenaline. Rex stood beside him, facing the woods in a protective stance.

Jackson shot a silent command to Dylan to check the house. *Lord, let Amelia have just missed her mother somewhere in there. Please.*

But there was no way Everly would ignore her daughter's cries.

As Dylan and Ridge stepped around him into the cabin, Jackson rocked the little girl back and forth, shushing her softly until her hysterical sobs eased into hiccups.

Although Amelia was still teary, Jackson needed answers if he was going to rescue her mother. "Okay, baby." He spoke into her dark hair, so much like her mother's. "Can you tell me what happened? Why you're crying?"

It seemed as though Amelia curled into an even tighter ball. She said nothing for so long that Jackson began to wonder if she'd ever speak again.

Finally, she sniffled. "I…was in the shower. And I got dressed. And I got a tangle in my hair." Her tiny hand reached up to the back of her head, where it looked like a bird had nested and then flown away.

Her voice was so small and scared. All she'd wanted was her mother, the one who had always been there when she needed her. "And when you went to look for your mama, she wasn't in the house?"

"I could hear a lady talking to her outside, and it wasn't nice words." Amelia shuddered. "Nobody was here. Not you or Rex or anybody. And I got scared. I tried to be brave but..." Her inhale fluttered. "I came on the porch but Mama was gone. And then I..." Tilting her head back, she pulled away and turned her tear-streaked face toward Jackson's. "I shouldn't have screamed."

He pulled her close. "You did the exact right thing. That way, I knew to come and look for your mama and to protect you. That's my job."

With a whimper, she nodded and snuggled into his chest again. "Did you see or hear anything when you came out on the porch?" If she'd heard a woman's voice, it was likely Kassandra was nearby. Maybe Amelia could give them some clue as to which way the women had gone.

Amelia shook her head but then she suddenly straightened and pointed to the left, away from the path Jackson and Dylan had been on. "I thought I saw something over there, but it was a shadow. I think." Her face scrunched up.

Every muscle in Jackson's body ached to rush into the forest in the direction Amelia had indicated, but he was torn. He couldn't leave the little girl behind.

But he couldn't leave Everly out there to fend for herself at the hands of a killer. As sharply as Amelia's cries had pierced his heart, the thought of losing Everly drove the knife in deeper. She meant the world to him. So did her daughter. If he lost one of them...

It was a pain he couldn't even begin to imagine, one so intense it nearly stole his breath. He cared about her more than he should, but there was no way to deny the feelings or to bury them any longer.

He loved her. He had for as long as he could remember. It had happened at some point while she was in the hospital, exhausted and fighting back from death after Amelia's birth. Sometime during their long, deep conversations that stretched into the night while Amelia slept in a plastic hospital bassinet between them.

That had felt like family. Everly had felt like his.

And so had Amelia.

He could no longer pretend he would ever be whole without them.

Standing, he turned toward the house and stepped toward the door, but Dylan came out and handed over a rectangular object.

Everly's field Bible. She'd had it at the other cabin, showing him something in the notes.

Dylan glanced at Amelia, who had her face buried in Jackson's chest. "I found it by the door."

There was no denying it.

Everly was gone.

FIFTEEN

Everly tripped over a root and tried to throw her hand out to find balance on the offending tree. With her hands zip-tied behind her, the motion threw her sideways, landing her on one knee on the packed dirt of the overgrown animal path that wound steeply down the mountainside toward the lake. Pain shot up her leg as her knee grazed a tree root.

It wasn't nearly as bad as the pain her heart had felt when her daughter had screamed with desperate fear. Amelia was alone, afraid... *Please, God. Don't let her wander into the woods after me. Please. Get Jackson to her quickly.*

Since Amelia hadn't cried out again, it was likely Jackson had already reached her. Maybe he and Rex were coming up behind them even now.

She should sprawl right here, pretend to be too hurt to walk. Maybe that would buy some time for—

The cold steel of the ever-present pistol pressed painfully into the hollow at the back of her neck. "Get up. Now. I have no problem killing you, even if your secrets die with you." Kassandra Rennish's voice was sharp and angry, riding the razor's edge of desperation.

Despite her fear, Everly dug into the deepest parts of herself and found a few brave words. They might be her last. "You need something from me. I don't know what it is, but if you didn't, I'd already be dead. You'd have sent someone else to finish and never would have gotten your hands dirty."

"Maybe I just want to be the one who watches you suffer." Grabbing a handful of Everly's shirt, Kassandra jerked her up to stand, then shoved her forward. "You cost me a lot. Time, money, my organization… I'm starting over because of you. Believe me, if I'd realized you were in the house the day I watched your husband bleed out on your lovely hardwood floors, you wouldn't be here now, and I wouldn't be having these issues."

Kassandra was trying to upset her by talking about Noah, but there was no way Everly would give her the satisfaction. She forced the images of Noah's death from her mind and focused on putting one foot in front of the other, trying to ignore the pain that rocketed from her knee to her hip with every step. She had to be brave even though her insides quaked. To trust Amelia was safe with Jackson and out of reach of this awful woman. To push enough buttons to keep Kassandra Rennish off balance without her going after Amelia in retaliation. All that mattered was her daughter. And somehow, if sacrificing herself kept her daughter safe…

Lord, I don't want to finish that thought. Help me. Get me out of this alive. But above all, if the worst happens…guard Amelia.

Deep inside, she could feel the peace that came when she knew God had heard her. It was as though He reminded her of the ways He'd already protected her precious little girl. She'd survived those early days in the hospital as a preemie and had been safe all of these years, even as a killer plotted revenge.

She was safe now, because there was no way Jackson would allow anything to happen to the little girl he clearly cared about.

It seemed Jackson had always been there for her daughter in the dangerous times. Actually, it seemed he'd been there all of the times. That was the reason she'd written those letters to him detailing Amelia's milestones, although she'd never thought he'd have the chance to see them.

With Noah gone, Jackson had stepped in to support and protect in ways far above and beyond his assignment. It was as though God had known Amelia would need someone during Everly's illness and after the death of her father, and He'd provided.

Everly had needed Jackson then as well. She needed him now, too. If God would get her out of this, she'd tell him the truth.

She'd fallen in love with him.

Not that it mattered. Jackson's sense of duty would prevent him from staying by her side.

Everly ducked away from a branch that would have torn into her cheek if she hadn't been paying attention, earning another shove from Kassandra. "Keep moving."

If Everly had guessed right, they were winding along this animal path down toward the lake. A boat likely waited, one they hadn't been able to see in the growing darkness and the shadows of the mountains. If they got to that boat, then she was gone forever. "How did you know where we were?"

"I've known where you were since you took a dive off that bridge." Kassandra sniffed, arrogance practically oozing off her. "Your cop friend dropped his phone when he jumped in after you. I guess they gave him another one, but I could still link into the network and access his GPS." She chuckled. "He really shouldn't have used your daughter's birthday as his passcode. That was too easy."

Tears stung Everly's eyes. So Jackson had never forgotten them, either.

Kassandra pushed her again. "I've had help along the way, but I've been here all along."

I've been here all along. The words sent a chill through Everly. She'd never been safe. It had all been an illusion.

Worse, Amelia had never been out of harm's way. Nor had Jackson.

But God had been *here all along* as well. It was likely the reason they were all still alive.

Jackson, though… It would devastate him to know his missing phone was the avenue through which they'd been found. He'd never forgive himself if something happened to her because of him.

If only there was a way to tell him this wasn't his fault.

That would require surviving the next few minutes.

As much as she'd feared this moment for years, the calm she felt shocked her. It was as though she stood watching from a different viewpoint, detached from the moment, pulling the strings on the puppet that was her body. It was a bit unnerving, but the disconnect was also keeping her sane.

Tough to say if it was fear or if it was God. Or both.

At a bend in the trail, a fallen tree blocked their way. Everly stopped and took in the massive evergreen that lay across the path. In the near distance, lake water lapped the shore with an oddly soothing sound. "You probably climbed that thing on your way up, but I can't climb over it with my hands behind me." There was no way. And the narrow space between the tree and the trail would never be big enough for her to slide beneath, particularly bound as she was.

"Doesn't matter." Kassandra grabbed her shoulder and turned Everly to face her, backing her roughly against the tree before she stepped away. "We'll be parting ways here."

For a half second, hope caught fire in Everly's chest. Was this really going to end with her still alive? Was this some sort of sick threat? A game?

Face-to-face for the first time with the woman who hated her literally to death, Everly studied Kassandra's features. Prison had hardened her, etching deep lines across her forehead and dark circles beneath her eyes. Her cheeks were hollow. She'd once been a beautiful woman, charming and friendly.

Or so Everly had thought. "Noah trusted you. He loved working for you." Until he'd found out what was happening behind the scenes.

"Then he should have kept quiet about what he was never supposed to know." Kassandra shrugged one shoulder, causing the barrel of the pistol to rise, then lower slightly before centering again on Everly's chest. "It was obvious when he found out the truth. He distanced himself from me. It didn't take much time to discover he'd gone to the cops and was planning to turn on me. When I found the evidence of his betrayal, I took care of the problem before he could do me any more harm."

"What do you want from me?" Everly's voice was calm. "Seems to me your bigger issue ought to be with your partner, who took off with your money and what was left of your organization." During dinner, Jackson had filled her in on what might be driving Kassandra's desperation.

Kassandra's nose twitched as though Everly's words held a stench only she could smell. "I'll find him. But you were the easier target. And you're the one who holds the key to putting everything back together again."

Tension settled across Everly's shoulders. She had no key. No nothing. "Noah never told me anything. I can't help you." As soon as she spoke, Everly winced. If she'd have kept her mouth shut, she would have bought time for Jackson and Dylan to find her. Instead, she had destroyed the one misconception that might keep her alive.

Waving her free hand dismissively, Kassandra shook her head. "You're lying."

"What do you want to know?" If nothing else, she could bluff her way through this, keep talking long enough to give herself hope of survival.

"Noah talked about you all of the time. I know he told you everything. You two were close. Too close, really."

No such thing in a marriage. "If he told me everything, then why not kill me when you killed him? Make sure I never talked?" That, at least, would have made sense.

"Anything you could say against me that Noah told you would be hearsay. I needed you alive back then to see if you knew where he'd hidden the evidence and how much he'd actually found, but you witnessed

Noah's death and went to the police before I could reach out to you."

Reach out? As though they were going to have coffee together? This woman had lost her mind.

"And then, I realized… If Noah told you everything, then you would know where he hid the documents he copied."

Everly couldn't stop her eyes from widening. "If he had any documents, he turned them over to the FBI." And if she'd known where they were, she'd have done the same. Clearly, Kassandra wasn't thinking with a rational mind. Fear and anger were clouding her common sense.

"Oh, he had them, but he never got the chance." Kassandra took one step closer, her eyes narrowing. "I know those documents are out there, and I want them. With the information in them, I can access money Dale didn't know I had. I can resume supply chains without having to start from the ground up." Another step closer. "And I can prevent you from ever turning them over to the FBI if I'm caught again."

She knew nothing about any documents, but she'd have to start bluffing if she wanted to stay alive. "Okay. Fine. But I have to take you. Where he hid them, there's a biometric lock." Those had better exist outside of the movies. For all she knew, they were science fiction.

Kassandra cursed. She considered her next move for a long time before she gestured toward the log with the pistol. "Then let's get moving. I've got a boat—"

In the distance, a dog barked and a second joined in.

Everly inhaled sharply. Help was coming.

Muttering more curses, Kassandra steadied the gun. Her intent was clear in her eyes.

She knew Jackson was on the trail and Everly would slow her down.

There would be no chance to bluff. Everly's time was up.

For the first time since he'd heard Amelia scream, Jackson's heart beat again.

As Ridge barked at the head of the animal trail Amelia had indicated, Dylan gave him a curt nod and let the K-9 have the lead. Ridge, a tracker, had made a slow inspection of the shirt Jackson had brought out from the house, then had immediately followed a scent trail to the edge of the forest, barking once to indicate he was onto something.

As though he understood the situation, Rex had answered.

Amelia had been right about the shadows in the woods. The little girl was now inside with Isaac and Freddy, who had been the first to arrive after his frantic all-call to the team. Amelia was familiar with Isaac and his partner, and had seemed comfortable with them.

Jackson prayed they were on the right trail, and this wasn't a ruse for Kassandra to double back and take the girl as leverage against Everly. Dylan had notified the rest of the team, and backup was currently on the way from multiple areas of the park as well as from the WITSEC team that was on the way to retrieve Amelia and Everly. Whatever this play of Kassandra Rennish's was, it would be her last in this game.

This ended today. *Let it end with Everly alive and safe, Lord.*

He couldn't think about that now. As Dylan and Ridge led the way up the trail, Jackson followed with

Rex, focused on the mission at hand. They needed to catch up to the two women, who had at least a ten-minute head start. One minute at a time, one step at a time, he was going to track them down and bring this to a close so Everly and Amelia could be safe again, even though it would mean they'd leave with the WITSEC team once Rennish was in custody.

Rennish's apprehension wouldn't change much. These past few days had proven they would never be safe as long as Kassandra Rennish was alive, no matter how securely she seemed to be locked away.

Could he leave everything behind to go with them? Did he dare—

No. One step at a time. One moment at a time. That was for later. In the future. This was right now, and his head needed to be squarely in the heat of the moment. This was how he'd lost Lance Carnalle, being distracted by Everly and Amelia. That could not happen again.

They were only a few hundred yards in, and Jackson could see the broken branches where the two women had pushed through ahead of them. Even without Ridge leading the way, it would have been relatively easy to tell they'd stayed on this trail.

The light grew dimmer as the shadows deepened with sunset. It would be full dark soon, and they had to find Everly before then. Plunging into the woods blindly would be the most dangerous game they could play. Not only would they be unable to see if Rennish or one of her skeleton crew lay in wait, but they'd also face nocturnal animals or risk attack from mother bears protecting their young in the night. If they didn't reach Everly in the next half hour, the chances they'd ever find her were slim to none.

He wanted to shout that they needed to go faster, but he bit his tongue so hard the pain made him wince. Any excess noise might alert Rennish that they were close.

The thick underbrush and low-hanging limbs coupled with the twilight to make a faster flight through the woods dangerous. One of them could be taken out by a root or a branch, then they'd be no good to Everly, instead waiting for their own rescue. He settled for the brisk pace they'd already set, hoping against hope Everly had managed to slow Kassandra down.

At a barely discernible fork in the trial, Ridge sniffed the ground before he took the left trail down to the river, ignoring the right-hand path that wound up the mountain.

"She has a boat." Dylan muttered the ugly fact, and it landed like a rock in Jackson's stomach.

A boat meant Kassandra could land anywhere on the lakeshore and take off with Everly, leaving no clue which direction they'd gone.

He stopped. They needed air support. "Go ahead. I'll catch up." Pulling his cell from his pocket, he dialed the chief. "I need a helo. We think Rennish has a boat. If she gets on the lake and we don't have eyes above to track—"

"I hear you." Donovan's voice was grave, and it was clear from the sounds in the background that he was in his SUV, likely headed their way. "I'll put a call in and see what we can do, but we'll have to get it in the air fast. They're going to balk at going up in full dark."

"Call in a favor." Jackson killed the call and pocketed his phone. He'd hear about his gruffness later, but right now he didn't care.

He'd taken only two steps when a gunshot cracked

against his eardrums, the sound so abrupt and horrifying that it skittered his feet backward two steps. *Everly.* Her name screamed from his lungs but stuck on the sudden pain in his chest.

No. No. No.

The only reason a gun would be fired up here was if Kassandra Rennish had fired it because she'd heard them coming and had decided having Everly as a hostage was not worth getting herself caught. *Jesus, please. Please. Not Everly. Please.*

Rex strained at the leash, eager to catch up to Dylan and Ridge. The sounds farther up the trail indicated the other pair had sped up.

Dodging branches and roots, Jackson raced forward, letting Rex have the lead as he stayed close to the trail of the other K-9.

A woman's pained scream raged through the trees. He couldn't tell who'd cried out but the sound chilled his blood.

New noises drifted to them as they rounded the bend to find a massive fallen tree blocking the trail.

Dylan stopped and reached for his weapon.

Jackson raced up beside him.

Everly. She scrambled to stand, her arms bound behind her. As she did, she backed toward them.

Jackson and Dylan drew their sidearms, but Everly was between them and Kassandra Rennish, who wobbled on her feet, the pistol unsteady in her hand as she tried to aim it at Everly.

What had happened here? Why was Kassandra wounded if she had the weapon?

Reaching down, Jackson unclipped Rex's leash. It was time for his partner to intervene.

"Rex. Attack."

As though he'd been fired from a rifle, Rex leaped forward, all of the sheathed energy in his muscles unleashing as he covered the ground in an instant and lunged at Kassandra Rennish, knocking her onto her back. The pistol flew sideways, landing on the pine needles with a dull thud.

As Rex passed, Everly dropped as though she was trying to make herself as small as possible.

Rex planted himself on top of Kassandra, his teeth fierce and his growl a threat to her life.

Jackson didn't call him off. He turned to Dylan. "Take her into custody." Without waiting for Dylan to move, he raced for Everly, who was struggling to get back to her feet. He knelt beside her. "Be still."

Everly froze, her chest bent over her knees. Her breathing was heavy enough to make Jackson's job tougher. Pulling his knife from its holster, he sliced through the zip ties, wincing at the bloodied marks left behind on her wrists, then helped her up and pulled her away from Rex and Kassandra.

"Rex. Stand down." Dutifully, Rex backed away from Kassandra, still keeping a watchful eye as Dylan rolled her onto her stomach and cuffed her.

Kassandra cried out weakly.

"Rennish has been shot. There's blood. Lots of it." Dylan looked over his shoulder. "She needs medical attention. Now."

Jackson scanned the trees, shielding Everly from a potential hidden shooter. "Who shot her?"

"She shot herself." Everly's voice was shaky.

What? Jackson shook his head once, clearing his mind so he could call for medics.

As soon as he had confirmation, he felt his shoulders sag. Everly was safe. He pulled her to him, and she melted against his chest, shaking. "What happened?"

"She was going to kill me." Everly's words muffled against his shirt.

"I know." Planting his forehead on the top of her head, he held her against his chest, never wanting to let her go. It was over. "How did she shoot herself?"

"She had me backed up… She was going to kill me and run. She wanted some documents Noah had but I didn't know where they were. Then she decided she couldn't outrun you with me. So when she aimed and got ready to fire, I dove. And the bullet ricocheted off the tree or a rock? It…" The words drifted away on heavy sobs.

"It's okay. You don't have to talk about it now." He tightened his grip on her and let her cry. She'd have to repeat the story often enough in the coming days. He could read it later.

After the report was filed.

And after WITSEC whisked her away from him forever.

SIXTEEN

Jackson sat on his desk and tapped his heel against the metal front. Not loud enough for anyone outside of the room to hear, but it was enough to keep the office from being entirely too quiet.

Rex rested in a kennel in the corner, doing his best to gnaw the edges off an industrial-strength chew toy. He'd earned this time in his favorite spot in the headquarters building. After saving Everly's life the night before, his partner could have anything his heart desired.

Jackson gripped the edge of the desk and leaned forward, then rocked back. Maybe the motion would jar loose some of the thoughts rolling around in his head.

Thoughts about Everly. Even about Amelia.

He'd still been in the forest gathering evidence and going over his story with the chief when WITSEC had arrived and taken them away. There had been no official goodbye. He'd held on to her as long as he could before duty called at the crime scene.

She'd hiked back to the cabin with Ruby, who'd arrived with the rest of the unit.

A rescue team had hiked out and transported Kassandra Rennish to Harborview Medical Center in Seattle. At last word, she'd undergone surgery for a bullet lodged near her spinal cord, and was recovering in the SICU under heavy guard. When she had recovered enough to move, she'd be tried for her jailbreak and the murder of Deputy Marshal Collin Anderson. Her handful of minions had been rounded up and were being handed over to federal authorities on multiple charges. Likely, they'd flip on her for reduced sentences.

But Rennish had proven prison wouldn't prevent her from being a threat, which meant Everly still lived in danger.

At this point, Everly and Amelia were probably already in DC being coached on their new identities. How was Amelia handling it? She'd been rocked by their house burning, though she'd had a point of reference to help her deal with it. But how did a four-year-old process being told she could no longer be the person she'd been since she was born?

"What's going on in here?" The words were followed by a soft tap on the door, and Ruby entered the room. "Sounds like you're forging steel." Her smile reached all the way to her deep brown eyes. "Not really, but I did hear the tapping when I passed by. You got something on your mind?" Shoving a pencil cup and a stapler out of the way, she sat on the desk beside him.

"I should be there." The words popped straight from his thoughts into the air.

"With the kid?" Of course Ruby would know what he was talking about. She generally did.

Jackson nodded. "She's going to have a hard time, and I know how the system works. I could explain. Help Everly help her understand. I mean, I was there when her life started, when she became someone she was never meant to be even from the moment she was born. I should be there now that it's happening again."

"So why aren't you?" The question was to the point, punctuated by the drawl that sometimes added weight to her words, like a Southern sage doling out wisdom.

"I'm an outsider now. WITSEC would never let me step in to—"

"I mean permanently. Why are you not going with them?" She nudged his shoulder with hers. "Jack, this is about more than that little girl. It's about her mama. Anybody with eyes can see that."

He wasn't going to argue. He did love Everly. Loved her to the point it made him feel hollow to know she was gone. But he couldn't uproot his whole life on the off chance she'd accept him. And marriage to someone in WITSEC came with its own series of trials and complications. He'd watched relationships fail under the stress. There was no way he'd do that to Everly and Amelia.

The last thing he wanted to do was fail them, even though he already had. "I messed up, you know. Twice." Jackson dragged his hand down his face, wishing he could forget his mistakes.

"I've told you before, you aren't responsible for the witness who got killed. He chose to put himself in a place where he'd be found. That's not on you."

"Losing my cell phone is on me." He spat out the words. The chief had told him how they'd been tracked. The assassin Kassandra had sent had found his cell phone on Pony Bridge after he dove in to rescue Everly. They'd cracked his password and not only tracked their movements but had sent the text to Owen. He didn't understand all of the logistics, but he knew enough to understand if he'd realized he hadn't lost his phone in

the raging river, that it had dropped onto the bridge before he'd dived in to save Everly, she and Amelia never
would have been tracked by Rennish.

"I heard." Ruby nodded in sympathy he'd rather she
not offer. "That had nothing to do with inattention. It
could have happened to anybody. You were focused on
saving a life, and you'd have jumped in that river after
any person, not just Everly, with the same results. It
was a fluke your phone didn't fall into the river, but it
wasn't your fault."

Maybe. Maybe not. He didn't want to talk about it
anymore. "There's more to it." Jackson sniffed, trying to
deflect Ruby toward more practical aspects. "I have this
job. Rex. The team. If I go to…" He shrugged. "Who
even knows where they're headed next? If I tag along,
I can't be in law enforcement ever again. I'll have to be
someone completely different."

"But you'll be someone different with *her.*" Ruby slid
off the desk and stood in front of him. "Is she worth
giving up everything?" Holding up a hand to keep him
from answering, she glanced at her watch and sighed.
"You can answer me later. We have a team meeting in
five."

Jackson watched her walk out the door as his phone
buzzed, probably with the text about the meeting. Did
he love Everly more than anything else? Even his own
life? This probably wasn't what Jesus was talking about
when He said the thing about greater love and laying
down his life for his friends, but still…

Did he love Everly enough to lay down this life for
her?

He walked over and scrubbed Rex's ear before he
closed the kennel door and locked it, looking down at

the K-9. "Maybe they'll let me take you with me, part-ner, even though you aren't quite to retirement age."

Rex looked up at him with a head tilt that seemed to say he understood, then he attacked the toy again.

Okay, then. His partner was cool with anything, so he could admit it.

Yes. He did love Everly that much. And as soon as this meeting was over, he'd talk with the chief about what came next.

By the time he walked into the conference room, most of the team was settled around the tables. He took a seat beside Ruby, giving a quick nod at her silent question.

She pumped the air with her fist, then dropped it quickly when everyone looked at her. She simply re-sponded with a smile and a wave before turning her at-tention to the chief as he walked in. He briefed the team on the roundup of Kassandra's few henchmen and on Everly's transfer to WITSEC.

He sobered and leaned forward, his fingers pressed against the tabletop. "Brady Carpenter, one of Rennish's associates, laid out how they found Everly Lopez and her daughter in the first place." He held up a printed page bearing a photo. From his seat, Jackson couldn't make out the picture. "Without her knowledge, Everly appeared in a national news story about flooding that hit the parks last year. The footage hit the fifteen-minute rotation on one of the cable news channels and, of course, it aired on one of the televisions in Rennish's prison. With the footage on loop for nearly twenty-four hours, Rennish eventually saw it and contacted one of the few who were left in her organization. There was enough information in the segment for them to realize she was a graduate student and to determine where she was in school. We're still working out details, but it seems they were able to tap into Everly's student email and to track down more intel from there."

Something didn't make sense. "Why kill Anderson?" If they'd tracked Everly to her college, there was no need to murder the agent.

"Collin Anderson made a habit of keeping an eye on his witnesses from a distance. Apparently, some of Rennish's men had been surveilling Everly for some time and Anderson caught on. He approached them and tipped his hand, so Rennish took him out and accelerated her plan to get to Everly."

Grief twisted Jackson's stomach. It sounded as though Anderson had been an above-and-beyond marshal, but even he hadn't been able to stop Everly's nightmare.

The chief set the paper aside. "His funeral will be in Seattle with honors next Wednesday, and I'll have details for anyone who'd like to attend."

Jackson wanted those details. He owed a debt of gratitude to the man who'd kept Everly safe.

Honestly, he needed to be out of this room. Now that he'd made a decision, getting to Everly had him on the edge of his seat, ready to bolt the instant the chief released them. He'd worry about his belongings later. All he wanted was to reach out to his contacts in WITSEC and to get to DC.

When he looked up, the chief was eyeing him as though he could read the thoughts running through his head. He started to speak, but Willow raised a hand quickly. "Do we have any updates on Mara Gilmore?"

The tension in the room amped. Their crime scene

investigator, still in hiding, was always a sore subject, with the team somewhat divided over guilt or innocence and how to proceed with the investigation.

The chief pulled his gaze from Jackson's. "Since she texted Asher that their father may be in danger, Asher and I will visit him in the memory care facility where he lives. Right now, that's all I'm going to say."

At the end of the table, Asher sat stone-faced. Jackson knew his relationship with his and Mara's father wasn't close. In fact, there was quite a bit of tension. Asher believed in his half sister's innocence, though, and that was likely enough to push him into a visit he'd prefer not to make.

Donovan scanned his tense team, then walked around the table and leaned against it, crossing his arms over his chest. "I think we've had enough heavy-heartedness for one day. Anybody got anything to lighten the mood?"

Beside Jackson, Ruby straightened. "Maybe not so much lighthearted as 'file it under something I wouldn't want to do,' but I read a news piece about a couple planning their wedding at the base of Mount Saint Helens. The way the volcano has been rumbling lately, I'm not sure I'd want to be that close."

On the other side of him, Isaac flicked the edge of the table, muttering, "Sounds like something Aubrey would do."

He'd never heard Isaac mention the name before. Maybe she was the ex-girlfriend Isaac had been talking about at the cabin, the one who'd dumped him by text.

Jackson watched Isaac from the corner of his eye. While he'd said the breakup had happened years ago, the way Isaac slumped now said it still brought a measure of pain.

"I don't know." Donovan glanced at his phone and frowned slightly, then looked at his team again. "There's no real sign she's going to erupt anytime soon, and it's beautiful up there." Before anyone could add further comment, he looked at Jackson. "Jack, meet me in my office. We have a few things to discuss."

Ruby elbowed him as the team rose, but Jackson ignored her. He had more things to say than the chief was probably ready to hear.

Everything smelled like wet smoke.

Everly ran her finger along the kitchen counter, where a fine black powder seemed to coat everything. While the fire had destroyed Everly's bedroom, the rest of the small house had suffered extensive smoke and water damage.

"It's pretty bad, Everly." Her landlady, Kesha Thompson, stood in the middle of the living room and surveyed the space. "The adjuster came by and he's working up some figures, but I'm not sure of the next step. I can release you from your lease, though, obviously. And I'll ask around to see if anyone else has a house you can rent."

"It's not like we could stay here anyway." Her room was destroyed, the afternoon sunlight streaming in through what used to be her ceiling. That was a quarter of the home's square footage right there. It was a good thing she'd dropped Amelia off at Tara's house. The little girl didn't need yet another trauma to imprint on her brain. Everly wrinkled her nose at the gray, muddy ash that coated her shoes. "I'll stay with friends until I can find something else, but I appreciate the help if you locate anything."

Kesha stepped carefully around a chunk of the ceiling that had fallen into the floor and gave Everly a hug. "Want me to hang around a while longer? Help you salvage what you can?"

"No. I just need a minute." So much had happened since she'd walked off the trail with Ruby just two days before. What she really needed was some time alone to process. She might as well do it right here in her ruined home. It looked like starting over was in her future, no matter how that looked.

"I understand." Kesha offered her one more quick hug, then headed for the door. "I'm going to make sure the water main is turned off, and then I'll get out of your hair. Call me if you need anything, okay?"

"Thanks, Kesha."

When the door closed behind her landlady, Everly dragged a kitchen chair from beneath the table in a corner of the living room. It had been largely protected from water and ash, and she sank into it, resting her hand on the plastic shoebox, filled with letters she'd written to Jackson, on the ruined table.

It had been tucked away in the top of Amelia's closet. Located on the far side of the house from the fire, her daughter's room had sustained the least damage. Mr. Ursa had been whisked away by federal marshals before the fire, and he was safely in Amelia's arms already, rescued from the stack of plastic storage containers the Marshals had delivered to Tara's house this morning.

The world still felt like a strange dream. Everything had been so surreal. She'd been at a small airport with the WITSEC team when everything had suddenly stopped. The Marshals had whisked Amelia and her into a small room without giving them any information.

The wait had been terrifying. Had they been found? Were they being tracked?

When a female marshal entered and presented the news that Kassandra Rennish had died from a blood clot after surgery…her whole life had changed. In a blink. Without warning.

Just like the first time.

She was free, but processing the feeling of it was impossible. For so long, she'd looked over her shoulder and worried. How did she act when the fear and the threat were suddenly gone? This must be what it felt like to walk out of prison after decades inside. Free…but what did that look like?

Especially when her freedom had come at the cost of another life. When she had no home to act as a refuge.

When the man she loved had let her walk away without a goodbye.

She dragged the box closer, leaving a streak on the soot-covered table. He was bound to know Kassandra Rennish had died and the threat to Everly's life was over. Yet there had been no phone call. No appearance. Nothing.

Did she leave him alone to live his life? Or did she reach out to him and confess her feelings? He'd come awfully close to telling her he felt the same way she did, but he always pulled away, citing the job.

Maybe that was the issue.

Well, she was going to ask him. For too long, life had dragged her around, forcing her into directions not of her choosing. She'd been a victim. It was time to take her life back, and she was going to start with Jackson Dean.

Grabbing the box, she gripped it with both hands and

stared at the blue lid. She'd reach out to him. Meet with him face-to-face. Tell him how she felt.

Then she'd give him the box and leave it in his hands. At least she'd know she'd taken charge and done all she could.

One more walk-through of the house to see if the Marshals had left behind anything of value and then—

"Everly."

Her heart slammed against her rib cage. Closing her eyes, she turned toward the front door...

Jackson stood there with Rex at his side, his face shadowed by the afternoon light that streamed into the house from behind him.

She gripped the box tighter. "I was on my way to see you."

"Were you?" Stepping deeper into the room, he shoved his hands into his pockets. His face was fully visible, and he offered her a weak smile that almost seemed...

Nervous?

In all of the time she'd known him, she'd never seen Jackson look so uncertain. He always valued control. Standing in front of her now, he looked like an uncertain little boy.

And she'd never loved him more.

He glanced around the room. "Why were you coming to see me?"

So many reasons. There hadn't been time to plan a speech in the five seconds between setting her resolve into place and his appearance at her door. It didn't seem right to just blurt out what she was feeling, although her tongue was ready with the words.

No. It should be more deliberate than that.

The edge of the box dug into her fingers, and her mouth quirked up into a smile. This. This was the thing she needed.

With a deep breath, she held the box out to him. "This is yours."

Arching an eyebrow, Jackson stepped forward with Rex trotting behind him and grabbed the other side of the box.

Everly didn't let go. They stood there, each holding onto the plastic, their eyes finally locked.

It was now or never. "These are the letters I told you about. The ones I wrote to you about Amelia."

"There's…" His voice cracked and he cleared his throat. His blue eyes were bright with an emotion that was hard to fully read. "There's more of them than I thought there would be."

There were more than she'd remembered. As time passed, she'd written about more than Amelia's milestones. She'd added thoughts about her day. Answers to prayers. Questions about faith. He'd become her closest friend, even though he wasn't present. As she'd written, she'd considered what he'd say if he read them. Based on what she knew of him, she'd found a lot of answers simply by pouring out words onto the page, wondering if he'd ever see them.

Everly sniffed, the sudden sting of tears at the back of her nose catching her by surprise. "Noah was…an amazing man. He would have loved his daughter so much. And I lost him." She pressed her lips together to stop tears that felt as fresh as ever.

"Everly…"

"No." She shook her head. If she didn't get everything out now, she'd never say it all. "We could have been assigned to any marshal out there. But when we needed you the most, God made sure you were there. I don't know how many other people in your position would have cared for us like you did. Would have befriended us like you did. Would have…have loved me enough to want me to know about Jesus and eternity and all of those things. Maybe a lot of them. Maybe just you."

He started to speak again, but Everly held up her hand.

At Jackson's feet, Rex tilted his head as though he was waiting for what came next.

"Jackson, God sent you. I will always love Noah. He will always be Amelia's father. But I know, now that I've had some time and some space to heal that… God sent you. Maybe for a season when Amelia and I needed you but…I think in my heart maybe it's not a season. Maybe it's—"

"Maybe it's forever?" Jackson's voice was husky. He took the box from her hands and held it in both of his, staring at the lid. Long moments ticked past.

Everly let him have as long as he needed, but she held her breath the entire time, waiting.

"Well." Jackson slid the box onto the table, then faced her again, reaching for her hands. "Well, I guess that saves me from making the speech I rehearsed all the way over here."

"Speech?"

"Yeah." He tugged gently on her hands, pulling her closer. "The one about giving you time to adjust to your freedom. Giving you space to decide what you want out of life. Letting—"

"I want you." She'd never been more certain of anything in her life. "Jackson, I love you, and I have for…a long time."

His smile was slow and easy, lighting a fire in his eyes. "Is that so?" His gaze dipped to her lips and up to her eyes again, asking a question she was more than ready to answer.

Everly raised up on her tiptoes and slipped her arms around his neck. "It's so." She tipped her face toward his. "I think, maybe…Amelia and I would like a new last name." It was bold, but she didn't care. What she saw in his eyes said his thoughts were running along the same track as hers.

"I think I can make that happen." This time, his kiss wasn't tentative and he didn't pull away. Instead, without words, he promised his heart was hers…and hers was safe with him. For good.

* * * * *

Don't miss Isaac's story, Threat Detection, *and the rest of the Pacific Northwest K-9 Unit series:*

Dear Reader,

I hope you had a great time running around Olympic National Park with Jackson and Everly (and that cutie, Amelia, and the best boy, Rex). I also hope you are enjoying the other books in the Pacific Northwest K-9 series. This is an amazing group of writers, and I am so blessed to work with them. The emails we've exchanged have been fun, challenging and encouraging. Let's do this again soon!

When I started the story, I wasn't sure what God had for me to say. But as I wrote, I began to consider how I'd feel if I found myself in Everly's situation. I'd be angry. So very angry.

Bad things are going to happen to us. I wish I'd learned sooner that, when those seasons come, God's okay if we get angry with Him. In my own times of *why* questions and frustration, I've learned that the worst thing I can do is to try to force down the feelings. God is big. He can handle it when I'm upset. In fact, He knows how I feel and He meets me in the dark places. I'm so glad.

When you're hurting or scared or just plain furious, God already knows. He wants you to talk to Him about it, even when the talking isn't pretty. Guess what… He loves you. He wants to have a relationship with you. Sometimes, relationships are messy, but that's okay. He's always there. And as it came to Everly and Jackson throughout the book, He is very interested in listening and in making beauty from the ashes.

Until next time!
Jodie Bailey

THREAT DETECTION
Pacific Northwest K-9 Unit • by Sharon Dunn
While gathering samples on Mt. St. Helens, volcanologist Aubrey Smith is targeted and pursued by an assailant. Now Aubrey must trust the last person she ever thought she'd see again—her ex-fiancé, K-9 officer Isaac McDane. But unraveling the truth behind the attacks may be the last thing they do...

HIDDEN AMISH TARGET
Amish Country Justice • by Dana R. Lynn
When Molly Schultz witnesses a shooting, the killer is dead set on silencing her and comes looking for her in her peaceful Amish community. But widower Zeke Bender is determined to keep Molly safe, even if it puts him in the killer's crosshairs...

SAFEGUARDING THE BABY
by Jill Elizabeth Nelson
When Wyoming sheriff Rylan Pierce discovers a wounded woman with an infant in a stalled car, protecting them draws the attention of a deadly enemy. Suffering from amnesia, all the woman knows for certain is that their lives are in danger...and a murderous villain will stop at nothing to find them.

DEFENDING THE WITNESS
by Sharee Stover
As the only eyewitness to her boss's murder, Ayla DuPree is under witness protection. But when her handler is murdered, she flees—forcing US marshal Chance Tavalla and his K-9 to find her. Can Chance keep Ayla alive along enough to bring a vicious gang leader to justice?

DANGEROUS DESERT ABDUCTION
by Kellie VanHorn
Single mother Abigail Fox thinks she's found refuge from the mob when she flees to South Dakota's Badlands...until her son is kidnapped. Now she must rely on park ranger Micah Ellis for protection as they race to uncover the evidence her late husband's killers want—before it's too late.

RANCH SHOWDOWN
by Tina Wheeler
Photographer Sierra Lowery is attacked by her nephew's father, demanding she hand over evidence linking him to a deadly bombing. Given twenty-four hours to comply, she turns to ex-boyfriend Detective Cole Walker, who is sure his ranch will be a haven...only for it to become the most dangerous place imaginable.

LISCNM0623

Get 3 FREE REWARDS!

We'll send you 2 FREE Books plus a FREE Mystery Gift.

FREE Value Over **$20**

Both the **Love Inspired®** and **Love Inspired® Suspense** series feature compelling novels filled with inspirational romance, faith, forgiveness and hope.

YES! Please send me 2 FREE novels from the Love Inspired or Love Inspired Suspense series and my FREE gift (gift is worth about $10 retail). After receiving them, if I don't wish to receive any more books, I can return the shipping statement marked "cancel." If I don't cancel, I will receive 6 brand-new Love Inspired Larger-Print books or Love Inspired Suspense Larger-Print books every month and be billed just $6.49 each in the U.S. or $6.74 each in Canada. That is a savings of at least 16% off the cover price. It's quite a bargain! Shipping and handling is just 50¢ per book in the U.S. and $1.25 per book in Canada.* I understand that accepting the 2 free books and gift places me under no obligation to buy anything. I can always return a shipment and cancel at any time by calling the number below. The free books and gift are mine to keep no matter what I decide.

Choose one: ☐ **Love Inspired Larger-Print** (122/322 BPA GRPA)   ☐ **Love Inspired Suspense Larger-Print** (107/307 BPA GRPA)   ☐ **Or Try Both!** (122/322 & 107/307 BPA GRRP)

Name (please print)

Address   Apt. #

City   State/Province   Zip/Postal Code

Email: Please check this box ☐ if you would like to receive newsletters and promotional emails from Harlequin Enterprises ULC and its affiliates. You can unsubscribe anytime.

Mail to the **Harlequin Reader Service:**
IN U.S.A.: P.O. Box 1341, Buffalo, NY 14240-8531
IN CANADA: P.O. Box 603, Fort Erie, Ontario L2A 5X3

Want to try 2 free books from another series? Call 1-800-873-8635 or visit www.ReaderService.com.

HARLEQUIN
PLUS

Try the best multimedia
subscription service for romance
readers like you!

Read, Watch and Play.

Experience the easiest way to get
the romance content you crave.

Start your **FREE TRIAL** at
<u>www.harlequinplus.com/freetrial</u>.